Finding Bigfoot
and
Other Stories

ISBN-13: 978-0-9994538-8-9
ISBN-10: 0-9994538-8-2

First printing, May 2019

Cover design: Jim Chueh, owner of Sprint Print, Decatur, Georgia, designed the cover artwork. Ron McCranie of "Silhouettes: See What I Saw" (706-331-7967) provided the digital artwork of Bigfoot. Lee Clevenger of ThomasMax Publishing designed the overall covers.

Published by:

tm

ThomasMax Publishing
P.O. Box 250054
Atlanta, GA 30325
thomasmax.com

Finding Bigfoot And Other Stories

Susan Lindsley

ThomasMax

Your Publisher
For The 21st Century

Acknowledgments

I am delighted to say that this collection of short stories took first place in the ThomasMax Publishing literary contest. So thank you, Lee Clevenger and Preston Ward, for this honor.

Also, I am fortunate to have met Ron McCranie's family at the Georgia Wildlife Federation Buckarama (a wildlife show) and saw his silhouette of Bigfoot. Ron graciously provided me with a digital copy of Bigfoot suitable for this cover. Ron produces silhouettes of various animals which now decorate yards and homes across the States and into Canada.

My friend Jim Chueh, owner of Sprint Print in Decatur, has helped me over many years with various projects. For this book, he assembled the Bigfoot illustration with a photograph I had taken to form the illustration for the cover. Thank you, Ron and Jim.

Pat Blanks, a friend from school days, provided her eagle eyes to help locate any typos or grammatical errors. Thanks, Pat. Know that any that remain are ones I happened to add after your careful readings.

As ever, I owe thanks to my life partner Gail Cabisius for her unconditional support.

A Word from the Publisher

ThomasMax Publishing has sponsored an annual contest since 2006 at the Southeastern Writers Association's annual workshop on St. Simons Island held every June. Susan Lindsley has won this contest several times, including the work you hold in your hands now.

If you are – or aspire to be – a writer, writers' conferences like the one sponsored by SWA can help you learn the craft of writing from professionals. Having attended SWA's workshop for the past 20 years, I am a bit prejudiced toward it as one of the finest. I've long maintained it's "the most fun a writer can have without taking his clothes off."

For more information, check out southeasternwriters.org.

For C.D. Mitchell

Table of Contents

Other Books by Susan Lindsley

All books currently in print are available from ThomasMax Publishing.

Novels, Southern historical
    The Bottom Rail
    When Darkness Fell

Memoirs
    Blue Jeans and Pantaloons in YESTERPLACE
    Possum Cops, Poachers and the Counterfeit Game Warden

Biography
    Susan Myrick of Gone With the Wind
    The Lindsleys of Westover

Edited Collections of works by others
    Myrick Memories
    Margaret Michell: A Scarlett or a Melanie?
    Luther Lindsley: His Literary Works

Poetry
    O Yesterplace and other poems (out of print)
    Christmas Gift

Short Story collections
    Emperor of the United American States (out of print)
    Whitetails and Tall Tales

Specialty Book (Photograhy)
    Wildlife in Persimmon Paradise*
   * available in soft cover and deluxe hardcover)

FINDING BIGFOOT

At seventy-three, she remembered her first time using a portable climbing deer stand and being excited to be able to hunt somewhere other than perched on the ground or on a stump. Every time in the woods, she remembered that day, the fall, and its aftermath. Today she was on her way to visit the friend who rescued her.

She worried this visit might be her last. The doctor had been blunt. She might have a month, but no longer. Even the ride on the four-wheeler had been exhausting today.

How many years since the accident? For close to twenty years she had come out here on the evening of every full moon and brought a basket of apples, bananas and grapes. Sometimes a new knife, or an ax, but always a tin of matches and for the last twelve years, a dozen arrows with razor broadheads. Sometimes she saw him and they waved but never approached. If she did not see him, she knew he was there, somewhere in the woods, watching her as he had the pre-dawn she fell as the full moon dropped behind the pines in the west.

He had kept her alive for three days until the rescue team had found her. Three months later, when she was able to drive her four-wheeler, she had returned to the site of her fall at twilight as the full moon rose. She did not see him, but signs told her he was nearby. She left the first basket of fruit and a tin of matches that day.

Sabrina at fifty-two had been as confident as she had been at thirty. Opening day of deer season, she set out before dawn for the mile walk to her climbing stand overlooking a trail chopped with deer tracks. Down the first ridge, across the bottom, over the creek, up the next ridge and down to a poplar thirty yards above the trail beside the stream.

A week of scouting and finding heavy deer signs—scrapes pawed by courting bucks and trees rubbed free of bark where a buck had rubbed velvet from his antlers—had led her to this tree. Three days before deer season opened she had carried her new two-part climbing stand to the site, attached both sections to the tree and finger-tightened the wing nuts to the bolts as snug as she could.

She tied her equipment and her Ruger .44 magnum rifle to her pull-up rope. A large stone served as a step for her to get her leg over the rail of the stand. She sat on the upper section, strapped her feet onto the foot board and pulled the safety strap about her belly to keep from falling off the seat.

I'm not gonna be a statistic like that guy up the road who tumbled out of his stand and broke his neck cause he didn't have himself strapped in.

She began to climb: Stand up, pull up the seat. Sit, tilt her toes down and raise her legs to lift the foot rest.

Almost twenty feet up, she realized something was wrong. The blade holding her seat portion of the stand wobbled. The bolt on the right side protruded upwards.

Impossible. I got them as tight as I could.

She halted her climb, stood up and reached forward to tighten the wing nut. As she touched the wing nut, it fell.

The blade swung wide. The seat bounced against the foot section and dropped. She grabbed the tree. Tilted her feet forward. Mistake. Tilting her feet forward freed the stand's grip on the tree. The foot portion began to slide down. She slammed her feet flat and halted the slide.

Fifteen feet above ground, she looked down. Not a soft spot to land if she fell. A couple of dangers awaited: The large rock she had used as a step to get into the stand and the portion of the stand on the ground with the sharp edge of its blade up and an invitation to a severe cut.

I'll have to hug the tree like Norman told me he had to when I talked about getting one of these. He insisted I get one with a seat and foot part. Damn. I hope I can hold myself to the tree to get down.

I hope there's nothing else can go wrong.

She glanced at the bolt head on her right. Nothing wrong there. She turned her attention to the bolt on her left. The head protruded.

As she bent forward to reach for the wing nut under the blade, the bolt screeched and flew off.

The blade snapped free. The stand dropped.

When she came to, confusion and pain controlled her. *What in hell happened? Where am I? My legs. Gawd, my legs hurt.*

She lay on her back and remembered. Her stand fell. Her legs hurt, must be broken. She looked up, but the poplar tree wasn't there. Only some sort of shelter of rocks behind crisscrossed limbs that filtered sunlight.

Where's my pack? I got to find it, get my CB radio. Get help.

She started to sit up. Someone grunted behind her and a hand pushed her back down.

A hand. She looked. It wasn't a human hand. *A bear? Gawd, I'm gonna be a meal for a black bear? No way. I'm getting outta here.*

She pushed against the hand and tried to sit up.

Again, the grunt, and more pressure to push her down.

The pain in her legs overpowered her more than her fear of whatever was behind her. She wanted to thrash her legs, to throw away the pain, but when she tried to move them, she discovered she couldn't. *Feels like they're tied down.*

She lay back, closed her eyes, and sighed.

The hand tapped her shoulder and then came into sight in front of her. Massive, hairy, with long fingernails, the fingers gripped her water bottle, cap removed.

Another hand slipped beneath her head and raised her as the bottle was extended to her lips. She drank four swallows, the bottle was moved away, and her head was lowered.

That's no bear. I must be dreaming or it's a gorilla escaped from the zoo. Oh, dear gawd I hurt.

She closed her eyes and took a deep breath. *I musta broken my legs is why they hurt so much.*

The animal grunted and she felt something laid against her side. She turned her head and saw her pack.

"Oh, my radio. I can call." She lifted the pack onto her chest, unzipped the main pouch and began to rummage inside. She felt the radio, pulled it out and turned the switch to *on*. Squeals greeted her as she tuned the dial to channel eleven and the truckers. When she heard distant chatter she broke in and hoped they would hear her. "Breaker, breaker. This is Lady Hunter. I need help."

"You got the Ranger Rider. What happened?"

"I fell out of my deer stand and need help."

"I'm near Tickleboro. I'll pull off and tell the sheriff. You stay on channel eleven and someone will get to you. Roger?"

"Ten-four. Thanks, Range Rider."

"What you doing hunting on a Monday? You don't have to work?"

"Monday? No, it's opening day."

"What? You mean you fell on opening day? Saturday? Lady hunter, it's Monday. You been on the ground all this time?"

"I just came to. I think my legs are busted up. Tell the sheriff to get ahold of Jerry Hinson. He'll be able to find me."

"Roger that."

In the moment of silence, several voices came on to offer help. She tried to thank them all.

I've been here, dead to the world, for three days? Jerry didn't even know I wasn't home.

In less than a half-hour, Jerry's voice came on the radio.

"Lady Hunter, you read me?"

"Oh, thank God, Jerry. I fell out of my tree stand and need help. I can't get up."

"Where are you?"

"I have no idea. I was overlooking the marsh trail. I'm somewhere nearby."

"Nearby? You fell and you've moved?"

"No, I fell and somebody moved me. I don't know how far. Maybe get a bloodhound and you can find me. You gonna have to have a stretcher. No way I can walk out of here."

"I'll get a crew together and we'll be on the way ASAP."

"Thank you. I'll keep the radio on."

"Roger. Talk to you soon."

She laid the radio on her pack that still lay on her chest.

The hairy hand reached into view, lifted the pack from under the radio and laid it beside her. She twisted her head around to see who, or what, was behind her. And saw only something hairy. She lifted her free hand and waved a *come here* circle.

The animal moved around to her feet and she gasped. It –no, *it* was a he, she saw, as she looked upward to his face. He stood eight feet or taller, as wide across the chest as her pickup hood. His arms dangled like the trunks of twenty-year-old pines.

His lips curled slightly, a smile. She nodded and smiled. "Thank you," she said. "I know you can't understand me, but thank you. You have to be Bigfoot. Sasquatch. Everybody's scared of you. But you've been so kind to me."

She lifted a hand. The creature bent forward and touched her hand with his. He tilted his head from one side to the other and again smiled.

"Sabrina, this is Ranger Mike. We can't get Willie's bloodhound until late this afternoon. Don't you know where you are? Jerry said you've busted your legs."

"No, Mike. I can't be far from the marsh meadow trail. That's where the stand fell apart. But somebody moved me to a kind of hovel. I understand it's Monday. I fell Saturday morning."

"I've called a crew together. As soon as Willie gets here, we'll start out. It's supposed to rain, maybe sleet, by morning. You got your cold weather clothes on?"

"Just get here as soon as you can. I can't move and my legs hurt like hell."

"We'll find you. Keep the radio on."

The hours passed. Twilight came, and with it the cold. When she shivered, Sass, as she named him, brought small pieces of wood in and stacked it nearby. He was going to make a fire, and she watched as he struggled with sticks to create enough friction to generate a spark.

"No," she said, and waved her hand. She reached for the pack, lifted it, and reached inside for the small plastic bottle where she kept kitchen matches. She removed one and held the match up. "Fire," she said. His face contorted. She pointed to his woodpile and then to the match and repeated, "Fire."

She pointed to a twig and he handed it to her. About two feet long, the twig was dry, dead and brittle. She struck the match against the sandpaper on the bottom of the jar and held the flame to the end of the twig. Flame flared on the stick but sputtered and went out. She handed Sass the container. He mimicked her, struck a match and pushed the flame into the duff he had been trying to light.

The duff caught, and the animal pushed the flame under his small stash of kindling. The fire blazed.

Sass jumped up and roared his delight.

Twice in the darkness he left the shelter and returned with more firewood. The fire kept away the growing cold. Well after midnight, she heard the bloodhound in the distance.

Jerry was coming, with Willie and others to take her to the hospital.

She opened her pack and removed the knife in its sheath. She slipped the knife free and reached for a piece of the firewood. "Knife," she said, and began to shave the wood into kindling. She replaced the knife in the sheath and handed the set to Sass. He copied her actions and shaved a pile of kindling. He looked at her, nodded and grunted.

She handed him the now empty pack, and pointed to its insides. He placed the knife and the matches inside and pushed the pack toward her.

"No, it's for you," she said and pushed it back to him. His expression changed as if to say, "Me?"

"Yes," she replied.

Jerry whooped. He was getting close. She tried to yell back, but her voice didn't carry far with her lying on her back.

Sass rose, lifted the pack, stepped outside the shelter, and roared.

The radio clicked as Jerry thumbed his. "Lady Hunter? Sabrina? My gawd, what was that roar?"

"That sure sounded like a bear. It's near me. Y'all hurry on up here. Where are you?"

"Foot of Black Rock Ridge. Can you holler?"

She tried again to yell. Her voice could not carry twenty yards.

Outside, Sass roared again.

"We've got a line to you now. See you in a few."

The woods went silent. She thought she heard Sass moving outside the hovel, but wasn't sure.

Less than a half-hour later, she heard the rescuers blundering though the woods. Jerry called, "Where are you?"

"I'm here. Over here. In this hovel."

Jerry's face was the first she saw. Behind him gathered seven men and the bloodhound. The two EMTs pushed Jerry aside and knelt by her. One said, "Somebody sure did fix up your legs. I've never seen such a splint—old pine boards held in place with muscadine vines. Where's your hero?"

"Can you give me something for the pain and more water?"

"We'll do better." The EMT started an IV in a vein in the back of her hand. "Sorry about the hand, but it's too cold to get you out of your hunting clothes to use your arm. Just call this Kick-A-Poo joy juice. Hydration and pain meds. We aren't going to mess with those splints till we get you to the hospital."

"Who helped you, Sabrina? Why didn't he come down to get help on Saturday when you fell?"

She tried to shake her head, but the pain from the cut on her scalp made her flinch. *If I tell, and word gets around, somebody'll come up looking for Sassy. Somebody'll want to be a hero and prove Bigfoot exists and bring home his body. I can't. I just can't tell.*

She muttered, "Can't say who he was. He never gave me his name. Scruffy looking. Probably scared of people. A mountain man of sorts. A hermit, I think. At least he's not the Olympic bomber they're looking for."

The joy juice had her dozing in minutes. When she woke up in the hospital she was in a bed, new splints on her legs, and a bandage around her skull where the cut on her scalp had been taped closed.

The orthopedist said, "Whoever put on these makeshift splints must have some medical knowledge. For the long time you were without care, he probably saved your legs. He set the breaks and even plastered leaves and mud over those slashes. He sure knew about what natural materials to use. You are one lucky lady. Who was your caretaker in the woods?"

"I can't say, Doc. I really can't say."

No way I'm telling anybody. They'll call me crazy.

By turkey season, she was up and walking again, although slowly. Her first venture was back to the Marshy Meadow area, to see what was left of her stand.

The broken foot section lay in pieces lay on the ground. The seat was still intact. *Glad I bought pliers and wrench. They won't come loose.*

She attached the seat section to the tree by using the bolts and wing nuts she brought with her. She lifted it up as high as she could reach and tugged on the seat until the blade caught.

She pushed the tools into her pants pocket, removed the pack from her shoulder and laid it on the seat of the stand. If Sass were still around he would find it.

Two days later, she returned. The pack was gone.

Four days later, when she bagged her turkey, she cleaned the gobbler and left the fresh meat hanging on the stand.

She went uphill about a hundred yards and sat. Sass must have been watching, for he came out of the woods, looked up the hill, raised a hand, lifted the bird and walked away.

"I'll have to get him a bow and arrows," she thought as she headed home. "All I have to do is shoot a few times. He'll catch on."

Periodically she left other items he could use. An ax, ropes, a tarp. And replacements for all as time went on and equipment would become worn out.

When the wooden stand rotted, she hung up a metal one that the tree had grown around over the past fifteen years. With all of her visits, she never went deeper into the woods beyond the stand. She respected his privacy and he seldom showed himself.

When the cancer first hit her and laid her up for several weeks, she told her son Bobby she had been taking supplies to the mountain man who had rescued her years ago, but he wanted privacy and seclusion. She swore Bobby to secrecy and gave him instruction of what to take and where to take it. For three months, he had followed instructions and reported he never did see the fellow, but each time he went back the supplies were gone.

Today, she knew she would not need to depend on Bobby again. The tin of matches lay where she had left it. The basket had been overturned and lay on the ground, the bananas rotting, the remaining fruit gone to scavengers. The arrows had been scattered across the ground where their fletching blended with the autumn leaves.

Sass had passed by for the last time.

THE MOONSHINE TRIAL

Judge Benjamin Franklin Stone had no trouble staying awake as he drove miles along the pine-shrouded road into nowhere. *I swear when I get back to Macon, I'm going to have to challenge Tommy Davis to a duel for sending me off to this Podunk town that seceded from the county and calls itself Euphoria. And just a stupid moonshine case that should have gone to the county seat. Maybe if I take him some of the moonshine, boosted with dead skunk, he'll get the message.*

He stopped at a single-pump filling station where an elderly man shuffled to the Fleetwood town sedan. Stone cranked down his window.

"Fill 'er up?"

"I don't need gas," he said. "Just tell me where the courthouse is."

The man leaned both forearms onto the car roof. "Nice caddy. A thirty-seven, ain't it?" He did not pause for a reply. "You here for the trial?"

"Yes. I just need to know where this town has its courthouse."

"We ain't got one yet. They set up in the Baptist Church, down yonder." He pointed to a small white clapboard building a block away. Its bell tower rose above all other buildings. "You can't miss it. Everybody in town is there, 'cepting me." He laughed. "I didn't vote for that crook, and should they put me on the jury, they know I'd vote him guilty. So I ain't going."

"Thanks," Stone said. The old man patted the roof of the car and backed away. Stone drove toward the church. A dozen wagons were pulled into the shade of several oaks, and pickup trucks of various levels of rust double-parked along the street.

He parked on the grassless lawn as close to the church as he could get without risking the paint job on his two-year old vehicle when a local opened his own door. The pickup truck beside him carried a dent in the fender and was spattered with dried mud. *At least, the potholes are dry and I don't have to worry about mud all over my whitewalls.*

As he opened his door the odor of fresh manure struck him, and he glanced at the bay mare hitched to a one-horse wagon and making her deposit. *Haven't had to smell that since I left Tickleboro for college. Better watch my step.*

He slid out and decided not to bother with his suitcase or his judicial robe. It was brinjin hot and he wasn't about to sit with his robe over his suit. At home, with a dressing chamber, he could shuck down to his boxers and no one would know he was almost naked.

From the looks of the trucks and wagons, every farmer is here for the festivities. He chuckled. *Maybe all the bootleggers from the entire county.*

He entered through the front door, into a packed sanctuary.

The number of men in overalls let him know he was right about the farmers. The outnumbered town folks wore cotton shirts and chinos. Not a woman in the room.

All had come for the trial of their one elected official, County Commissioner Frederick Wilkes, for making shine. June 6 would go down in local history as the day the county commissioner had gone on trial for moonshining.

Folding chairs stood in two ranks to serve as a jury box. The judge would preside at preacher's podium, and two card tables provided desks for the trial attorneys.

Unlike Sundays, when the tall fans standing along the walls circulated ladies' perfumes, today the smell of manure, dirt and sweat floated in the sanctuary.

A fat man with a badge approached and said, "You the judge?"

"Yes."

"Well, Judge, I'm the law in this town." He grinned, tugged up his gun belt and pushed out his chest. His voice dropped to a whisper. "I didn't know nothing about that still till the federal man—"

Stone interrupted. "That's enough. I don't want to hear anything about this case except what's under oath." *Wonder if he was in on the still himself.*

"Yes, Sir." He slunk off and found a spot to sit in a pew.

Judge Stone took his seat, introduced himself, and asked the attorneys to do likewise.

"I'm Judson Wilkinson, for the defense," the tall sunburned man said. He was the town's only lawyer, who mostly drafted wills and on the rare occasion of a farm sale, he drew up the deeds. Without his own farm, he probably would have needed charity. He wore Dickie's pants held up with unneeded red suspenders. His tie-less shirt matched the brown pants. An ink pen had leaked a patch of black at the bottom of his shirt pocket. Judge Stone noticed Wilkinson's Red Wing boots wore a layer of manure-laced mud.

The prosecuting attorney rose and stated, "I'm Stanley Brookins and here from over in Toomsboro to see justice done." Stone swallowed his smile. This attorney was better dressed for the courtroom in gray flannels, white shirt and a bright blue tie. And highly polished black shoes.

Judge Stone called the room to order and *voir doir* began. To his surprise, both attorneys accepted the first twelve jurors called to the box. He shrugged, studied the men and then turned his attention to the two attorneys.

"You both accept these men without question?"

The defense attorney said, "Oh, yes, Your Honor. I've known every one of them all my life. No need for me to ask anything."

"And you?" He looked at the prosecutor.

"I don't know them," he said, "but I know the reputation of the citizens here. I'm sure we have a group of honest and upright men in the jury."

Just playing to the jury. "Very well. Proceed."

Prosecutor Brookins called the arresting federal officer, Brandon Monroe, who was sworn in.

"Now, Agent Monroe, did you or did you not find the defendant at an operating still?"

"I did."

"And did you or did you not therefore bring charges against him that led to his trial?"

"I did."

"That's all I have, Your Honor."

Defense attorney Wilkinson stood, hooked his thumbs in his suspenders and strolled back and forth as if deep in thought.

"Did you or did you not destroy the still?"

"I did."

"Did you or did you not pour all the contents onto the ground?"

"I did."

"Did you or did you not taste any of the contents?"

The witness turned red and shouted. "I most certainly did not."

"Then howcome you think he was making whiskey if you didn't taste it?"

Everyone in the room laughed.

So did the jury.

Judge Stone had to cover his face to hide his snicker.

Wilkinson said, "That's all I have, Your Honor."

"Any re-direct?" Judge Stone asked Brookins.

The prosecutor stood, glanced at his opponent, and shook his head. "No, Sir."

"Call your next witness."

"He's it, Your Honor."

"Well, who does the defense call?"

"We don't need any witnesses," Wilkinson said.

"Very well. Are you prepared for your summary to the jury?"

"Yes, Sir," the two answered in unison.

The prosecutor stood and walked over to the jury. One by one he met their gaze and nodded. "Well, we have the word of the most honorable of men. A federal agent of the Alcohol, Tobacco and Firearms agency whose duty is to keep the country safe from all three of these dangerous substances. Agent Monroe swore under oath he caught our friend here," he pointed to the county commissioner, "at an operating still. You don't need any other evidence to find him guilty. It's your duty to your country, to your state, and especially to your county to find the defendant guilty as charged. Forget he is your county commissioner. Forget he plans to run for the state house. Forget he owns the only feed and seed store in thirty miles. Forget he is a deacon in his church. He is guilty as charged. He was caught at the liquor still and must pay his dues to the law. Same as anyone else. It's your duty to find him guilty."

The prosecutor sat.

The defense attorney stood, and the odor of fresh manure wafted through the room. Judge Stone waved his hand in front of his face and frowned. Wilkinson ambled over to the jury and studied the floor for a few moments.

As if suddenly noticing his boots, he stomped one toe to the floor and grimaced. "Oh, my. I apologize, Your Honor, Pastor. I didn't realize what I had on my boots. I didn't have time to clean them after I plowed the corn yesterday. I'll clean this up after the trial."

He paused as if waiting for the pastor or the judge to accept his behavior and the manure he had just deposited on the floor.

"Gentlemen of the jury, this is indeed a sad day for our home town. Here we have a man," he pointed to the federal agent, "who has come here and disrupted our community. Here is a man from the government. You know the government in Washington. It is evil. It takes our money and keeps it while all over our great nation people are going hungry. It used our own money to send people like this one down here to take even more. This man admitted he did not taste what he found in the woods.

How does he know it was whiskey if he did not taste it? How can he sit there and tell us he busted up a still when he provided no evidence? What government man tells us the truth? And what was he doing out in those woods in the winter? Was he poaching? Did this government man come down here to steal our game right out of our woods and decided since he couldn't find a deer he might as well just arrest our county commissioner? You all know Commissioner Wilkes. You voted for him. You know he doesn't moonshine. Why would he have to? He doesn't need money. He has the biggest store in town, where you can buy anything you want, on credit. Why, you can even buy bottles of whiskey. Store-bought whiskey. From Tennessee and Kentucky.

"No, Sir, he doesn't need to moonshine. Why, you all know moonshine can kill you. And you know a moonshiner will run off his whiskey even if a skunk gets into the mash. Not a one of you would buy moonshine. So howcome Agent Monroe who works for the government comes down here and tries to say our county commissioner is a criminal? Aren't most of the people in our Washington government somehow criminals? They don't do anything but sit around and talk and figure out how to get more of your money. Here you are down here trying to make a living. And that's all our county commissioner is trying to do with his store is make a living.

"You cannot believe this man," he turned and pointed to the revenue agent sitting at the table beside the prosecutor, "this Agent Monroe, who has no evidence of liquor being made. He didn't even taste it, for crying out loud.

"How can you believe him? First, he's out to say we are all a bunch of drunks who live on moonshine. Next, he'll say you can't have your smokes. Tobacco is bad for you. Smoking can kill you. Can kill your children. So next he'll take up all the tobacco out of our county commissioner's store and say our county commissioner is out to kill you by selling you cigarettes and Prince Albert? Remember, he's Alcohol, Tobacco and Firearms. Next thing Agent Monroe will be ordered to do is take your guns."

"Nooooo," rose with the force of a tsunami from the crowd.

Judge Stone let the roar die of its own accord.

The attorney continued. "If the federal government learns it can arrest a man who was taking a walk in his own woods and say he might have been making whiskey, what will this agent, this representative of the government, do next? You can't let him get away with such. If you do, you better go home and hide your tobacco and your hunting rifles. Especially when you know County Commissioner Wilkes is not guilty."

He sat.

The jury took only a half-hour to return its verdict. The judge asked for the written verdict, read it, raised his eyebrows, and handed the paper back. "Please read your verdict," he said.

The foreman accepted the paper and read, "We find the defendant not guilty because we know the government is out to take our smokes and our guns."

FLIGHT 1950

"Welcome aboard Flight One Nine Five Oh," the stewardess greeted each one as they boarded.

A lady on a walker asked, "Is this the plane to St. Louis?"

"Why, yes, it is," the stewardess replied. "By way of St. Augustine, however. We will refuel there."

The next passenger overheard and said, "I thought we were going to Daytona Beach."

" Oh, we are. With a brief stop in Dahlonega, however."

"I didn't know they had an airport there. I haven't been back to the college since I was graduated in 1951. I want a window seat so I can see the college campus as we fly in." The old man leaned on a cane and held his elderly wife's elbow with his other hand.

"A window seat it is for you, Sir. You can view your college campus from the air and on the ground after we land. And thank you for your service to our country during the unpleasantness with North Korea."

The old man smiled. "The first war we lost. And looks like we may be going back again. They never put me on *M*A*S*H*, but the war was a lot worse than what they showed on the TV program. It was nothing to laugh at."

"We well know, Sir. Take any seat you two wish."

He looked over the compartment and noticed for a plane of its size it didn't have many seats. There was leg room aplenty. Every seat on one side was by a window. And on the other side of the aisle were two seats together. The aisle was wide enough for two people to dance if the stewardess would just play the right music.

A couple boarded, each using a cane. She welcomed them and the husband said, "I'm a bit confused. The personnel at the check-in desk said this was the plane our tickets were for, but the departure board said it was going to Merritt Island. Our tickets are for Long Island, New York."

"You are on the right plane, Sir. Take any seats you would like. Or if you want to sit together, there is one more double seat for special couples."

The husband looked at his wife and grinned. "I get to hold hands with you like we did back on our honeymoon flight." She giggled and blushed.

He leaned a bit on his cane and kissed her cheek. "Let's take the last double seats." They hobbled down the aisle.

The stewardess called, "All aboard Flight One Nine Five Oh, for destinations south."

She closed the entry door and stood at the front of the passenger compartment. "May I have your attention please?" Everyone looked up and listened as she went through the routine of the oxygen masks and flotation devices.

"We've never had one of our planes fail or fall, so I want you each one to relax and enjoy the flight. First stop, Merritt Island."

The plane taxied to the runway and lifted into the sky. The passengers were amazed at how quickly they landed at Merritt Island.

The stewardess approached the elderly couple. They were holding hands and cuddling like teenagers at the drive-in back in the 1950s.

"This is your stop."

"We were going to Long Island."

"Isn't this where you two met, working on America's secret?"

"Well, yes."

"We have arranged a special tour for you here. A car is waiting for you. If you decide to go on to Long Island, we will pick you up on our way north."

Through the window the couple saw a wood-sided station wagon parked only feet from the stairway. The stewardess said, "Looks like your transport is a few years old, but I imagine the motor is as young as your hearts."

"Come on, darling. Let's take the tour. See how it's all changed since we were here. Besides I haven't seen a wagon like that since we courted in one."

They departed. The stewardess stood in the open door and watched as the couple reached the car. The old man looked inside, but there was no driver. He went around and opened the door for his aged wife and helped her get inside. He hobbled around and crawled under the steering wheel. He rolled down his window.

The stewardess smiled as she watched the tall blond youth drive away with a laughing girl beside him.

On to the next town to turn time around for the other passengers.

ONCE UPON A MIDNIGHT

She was deep into a dream about salmon fishing in Alaska when the knocking began. Five knocks followed by the screeched demand, "Open the door. Open the door."

She staggered from the bed and turned on the lamp. Midnight. She shook her head to try to wake herself up. The visitor continued. Five loud knocks and "Open the door. Open the door."

Clad only in her undies and her sleep tee shirt, she rushed to the front door. It was solid wood, one-inch-thick walnut with no peep hole, no sidelights, no way to survey the visitor.

"Who is it?" she called.

"Open the door. Open the door," came the reply.

"I'm not opening the door until you tell me who you are."

"Open the door. Open the door."

"Who are you? What's the matter?"

"Open the door. Open the door."

"Did you have car trouble?"

"Open the door."

"I am not going to open the door until you answer me. I'll call the sheriff if you just stand there and demand I open the door."

"Open the door."

"Okay, I'm going to call the sheriff."

She returned to her bedroom while the knocking began again and the voice kept demanding. She didn't bother with 911 since the sheriff was a friend and she had called his office to chat a few times. He was home asleep, but when the dispatcher answered, she said, "Hi, Carol. It's Sally Dickens. Somebody's at my front door demanding I open the door and he won't answer when I ask *who are you*. I hesitate to open the door when I don't know what's going on. Will you send one of the deputies over to see who this is and help him out of his troubles?"

"Andy's on patrol in your area. I'll have him stop by. You want the noise and lights?"

"Maybe not. Whoever it is might be scared and run and he might really need some help."

"Sure. Stop by for coffee when you come to town again. We need to catch up on gossip."

"Will do. Thanks."

Sally slipped into jeans and a sweat shirt to face the cold late-October night. She saw headlights through the bedroom window and went to the hall.

The visitor went quiet.

This time three knocks and Andy's voice, "Miss Sally, it's Deputy Andy."

She opened the door. The night was half-dark as clouds scuttled across the moon and dragged their shadows across her front lawn. *Midnight, dark and dreary. At least it's not a raven knocking on my chamber door.* "Hi, Andy. Thanks for coming out."

"I didn't see anybody when I drove up. I'll check around the yard. You okay?"

"Oh, yes, I'm fine. I don't understand. Whoever it is must have run off when you drove up. I saw your headlights from the window, but whoever it is should not run off from headlights. Please do check around."

"You stay inside and keep the door closed. I'll be back in a few minutes."

She watched while he went down the steps into the yard, then closed the door and threw the latch.

Two minutes passed. Five knocks and "Open the door. Open the door."

It wasn't Andy.

"Who are you?" she yelled.

Only the repeated knocking and the demand, "Open the door."

She darted through the house to the back door. From the kitchen window she saw Andy's light bouncing as he ran toward the house. She raised the window and yelled, "He's back."

"I heard him. I'm on my way."

She returned to the front hall. Out the window to her left, she saw the flashlight approaching. The knocking stopped.

Andy tapped on the front door.

She opened it. "Did you see him?" She stepped onto the porch with her five-battery flashlight and turned it around the yard.

"There wasn't anybody there. If I hadn't heard it, I'd have sworn you were having a nightmare. But somebody's here. I'll call for backup and we'll search the whole area."

"Maybe have them come out with lights and noise. That ought to scare away whoever it is."

Andy nodded and keyed his shoulder mike. "Carol, we have a problem out here. Whoever it is is hiding. I need backup to find him. I went to search the yard and while I was in the back yard, he returned to the front door and tried to get in again. Can you send out Jerry and Mike?"

"Will do. Want me to wake up Bill?"

Sally shook her head, "No, we don't want to get the sheriff up just for some vagrant who's probably just looking for a house to crash in or food or some such. I just don't want to open the door and find myself facing something worse."

"Okay. I'll send the others out. Give 'em about ten minutes."

It took barely five for Sally and Andy to hear the Sirens. Both vehicles drove up to the edge of the porch. The two deputies left the lights swirling colors into the night, scurried from their cars and ran up the porch steps.

Jerry said, "You got yourself a Peeping Tom?"

"Not peeping that we know of. Just knocking on the door and demanding to be let in and we can't find him. Let's spread out and search the entire yard for him or any signs or tracks where he might have run. Sally, you be okay here on the porch with our chase-em lights going?"

"Give me a minute and I'll get my .20 gauge and load it. It'll scare somebody even if I don't have to shoot, and if I shoot y'all come running."

"Okay," Andy replied.

She returned immediately, shotgun in one hand and three shells in the other and began running them into the magazine as she walked onto the porch. "I'm good," she said.

"Maybe he'll show back up and I can find out what the heck he wants."

But after half an hour of searching through boxwood hedges and across the five acres surrounding the house, they had found no tracks and no sign of anyone.

"Nothing," Andy said. "Whoever it is must be long gone by now. We couldn't find even a track."

"Thanks, fellows. Y'all go back to patrol and I'll go back to bed. Oh, no. Wait. I have some Krispy Kremes I bought late yesterday. Hold on, and I'll get them and some Cokes and we can visit a few minutes."

She leaned the shotgun into the corner of the front hall and hurried to the kitchen. Andy came behind her. "Need a hand there?"

"Sure. I'll grab the Cokes and make-do napkins. You take the donuts." She nodded toward the box.

They returned to the porch and the four of them sat and devoured the last eight donuts. The guys licked the remaining sugar from their fingers and wiped their hands on the paper towels she had brought out.

"Thanks," Mike said. "Call me any time you have donuts to spare."

"Me too," Jerry added.

"If you need us, you know where we are," Andy said. He smiled and continued. "And if your visitor returns, don't hesitate to give him a dose of that .20 gauge."

She laughed and the fellows left.

Sally turned off lights and returned to bed. She had not dozed off when the knocks came again. Same pattern of five knocks and the demand, "Open the door, open the door." Five knocks and the demand repeated.

He must have crawled under the house when he saw the deputies. Damn, why didn't I think of that before? She got up, pulled on her jeans, stormed to the hall, and reached for the thumb latch. She pulled her hand back, lifted the shotgun.

She stepped to the wall so she'd be behind the door when she opened it. She reached forward, flipped the thumb latch and jerked the door open.

The largest parrot she thought possible flew into the hall, landed on the upstairs banister and screamed, "Open the door. Open the door."

NEPTUNE'S REVENGE

Tsunamis

Janice perched in her wheelchair in front of the nursing home's reception desk where she could drink coffee and chat with the aides. She tried to ignore their TV which was always set to a talk show or to a soap opera. In the middle of a heated conversation between an adulterous husband and the wife who had learned of his misbehavior, the screen blackened, flashed white and *ALERT* ran in red letters across the screen.

A weatherman, the map of the Gulf of Mexico behind him, spoke: "Just in. Never before have hurricanes developed so quickly or so close together. In the Gulf, south of Texas, what an hour ago was only a small depression has developed into a hurricane and gone from a Category 1 to a Category 3 in the past thirty minutes. Near the Yucatan peninsula, another squall has also formed in the past hour and is already a Category 3 and it is sitting in place. Not moving. A third one has formed off the junction of Florida and Alabama. Absolutely no movement from any of the three, as if they are trying to decide which way to go. We can only hope they don't strengthen like Florence did."

Janice cackled. "Old Neptune's finally plotting some revenge. Every one of them is gonna get bad. Any one of them could dump a much rain as Harvey. Or flatten everything like Irma and Florence. I wonder which way they'll go."

Ellen, an aide, walked up as she spoke. "Miss Janice, you sound like you're an environmentalist."

"Oh, yes. I spent sixty years researching the ocean. Unfortunately, I saw it go from nearly pristine to a trash dump."

"What do you mean, *trash dump*?"

"You know a lot of beaches have closed. Even where I worked for years, back in Massachusetts, near Cape Cod. Truth is, coastal towns closed their beaches because of the pollution. If you didn't have a tetanus shot you had no business anywhere near a beach. Why, some of those grand hotels just dump their sewerage into the ocean as if they think it'll go away. Medical waste gets dumped. I walked on one Carolina beach for pleasure several years ago and saw all kinds of trash. Stuff you wouldn't think people would throw into the ocean—like tampons, diapers, metal beer cans, and glass and plastic bottles. Couples sat under umbrellas with coolers, and when they left, they just dropped their trash on the beach and walked off. Old Neptune is about to take his revenge. Turn the TV on the Weather Channel and I can watch it all."

"Well, you'll have to wait awhile. It's time for supper. You want your walker or want me to push you in the chair?"

"Oh, I feel like walking. You mind getting my walker?"

"Of course not." Ellen smiled. "Don't you run off now. I'll be right back."

She returned with the walker, helped Janice stand and they started for the dining room.

"What excitement! I want to sit with Tim tonight."

"I'll see to it."

The old lady's body shook with the strain of walking, her weight more on the walker than on her legs. But a smile lit up her face and deepened the parentheses around her mouth.

The two entered the dining room. She paused to find Tim, and when she spotted him she raised her right arm and waved. "Tim! Neptune's finally getting his revenge!" She grasped the walker again and charged across the dining room toward the old man. Tim rose from his chair as she approached.

"What do you mean, Janice?" He spoke with the diction of a native of the Maine coast in contrast to her soft South Carolina accent.

"Three, count 'em, three hurricanes right now in the Gulf. Just getting ready to slam into the land and tell us people to have more respect for the water that keeps us alive on this earth. Nobody cares for anything about the sea except the beaches they contaminate. They just don't care anymore."

Ellen pulled out the chair next to Tim and Janice eased her frail body onto the seat. The aide pushed her toward the table. Janice reached over her shoulder to thank the aide.

All through supper, Janice and Tim recounted their days as environmentalists and oceanographers, their years together at the Woods Hole Oceanography Institution, and the changes they had seen. They discussed the televised program showing the collection of trash that formed an island in the Pacific—everything from empty plastic containers to furniture. Both railed against the plastic bags thrown to the wind and sea by people who had no inkling sea turtles saw them as food, ate them and died.

Janice added. "And the manatees scoop up all kinds of trash when they feed on the bottom grasses. And it kills them."

"I sometimes wish the ocean could just throw it all back," Tim said.

"Well, come on to my room and let's watch the weather reports together." She laughed and added, "Maybe the storms will do just that down there in the Gulf. I've got a fifty-two-inch flat screen now, so my poor eyes can see it see real easy."

He joined her, and while she sank against her pillows in the bed, he relaxed in the recliner—a pair of teenagers about to watch their high school team win the state championship.

Janice clicked the remote and the screen opened to a talking head in one portion of the screen and the rest split into three views: Each showed the massive white band of clouds churning around a distinct open eye. Beneath each were a name and a wind speed: *Alma, 145 mph; Beatrice, 150; Caroline, 160.*

"Two of these storms seem to be a threat to the United States," the head stated. "But Caroline in the Gulf seems to be a threat to Mexico. We have received reports of cyclones in the far eastern Pacific which threaten Japan, the Korean peninsula and Indonesia. One in the Indian Ocean is headed toward India. All of these are Category 4 or 5. These storms are unprecedented. Never have there been such storms. Yes, maybe a line of two or three in the Atlantic spun off from Africa."

He paused, put a hand up to his ear and tilted his head as if to hear better. The screen behind him changed and showed a storm circle in the mid-Atlantic.

"Looks like another one has developed out of nowhere in the Atlantic, not spun off from Africa. Hurricanes don't normally form in the mid-Atlantic. This one did, however. It's moving directly west. I can't believe it is gaining strength in non-tropical waters. If it continues on this same course, it will hit Washington. It's almost as if the ocean is rebelling against the land of the earth itself. Or that God is ..."

An off-screen voice interrupted. "Don't be ridiculous, Sam. It's just a quirk of some kind, not a rational act of the ocean or an act of whatever God you worship."

The reporter glared in the direction of the voice, shook his head and looked back to the camera. Before he spoke again, a pale-faced man in headphones attached to wires he dragged behind himself entered the screen. His hand trembling, he handed a paper to the reporter and slumped off screen.

Janice laughed. "If they only knew, Tim. If they only knew. The ole ocean does indeed have a mind of its own. The Greeks and Romans knew and all before them. They respected the seas, feared the gods of the seas. Aren't you glad you took my advice when you retired and also came on out here to Montana?"

"Yes, but. You know there's always a *but* in anything you like in life. I do miss the salt air, but like you said, the skies here are about as wide as the ocean's. And just as varied. Maybe more so."

The announcer shouted. "This just in. From a satellite view of the west coast. The ocean is receding from our west coast. From Alaska all the way down… down below California, all the way to Chile, no, even to the tip of South America. The Pacific has receded… a mile. More than a mile."

The view changed to the satellite's eye-view and showed the three-mile stretch of ocean bottom. The wave came, rising higher and higher as it approached land.

"It's coming," he shouted. "Oh my God, no one can escape. The tsunami is… oh sweet Jesus. It's—it's—it's a half-mile high. It'll cover the west coast. No one can survive. Oh my God. It's worse than if the San Andreas fault had torn California off the continent. Oh, dear Lord."

The satellite continued to focus on the western United States, on the area between Los Angeles and San Francisco. The wave wore a white frothy crown and stood erect, the sunlight behind it glistening on the froth but unable to penetrate the rising waters. Objects riding inside the wave shadowed it to black. The wave reached shore, roared over the skyscrapers, continued through the cities and on toward the desert lands east of Los Angeles and toward the mountains of Nevada.

The talking head remained silent as the western U. S. became an extension of the Pacific.

Janice and Tim, like the rest of the world, remained silent as the waters thrashed the man-made structures and pushed civilization and life eastward. The flood slowed, stopped, and began to recede.

"Well, I never expected anything like that. They didn't even report an earthquake," Janice said.

"Like you said before, Poseidon is mad."

"You mean Neptune."

Tim laughed. "We don't need to argue Greece against Rome. I'd say both gods are a bit mad."

A new talking head came onto the screen. "This is Jason Drivers reporting. The tsunami has receded. It wiped out several miles of everything along the coast. But the satellite camera shows piles, and I mean high piles, of debris along the coast line. No beach is visible now. Just trash. It looks like man-made trash. Plastic bottles, ice coolers, furniture, half-rotten boats."

He paused and stared at the image of debris pushed more than a mile inland and heaped over the remains of the coastal cities.

"Just in. The hurricanes in the Gulf are moving. More than thirty miles an hour across the Gulf. One is headed to Texas, one to northern Mexico, one to western Florida. At their speed and from their diverse locations, they will strike almost at the same time. We have a report of another storm in the mid-Atlantic. It is developing rapidly and moving east, toward Europe."

At a knock on her door, Janice called, "Come in," and turned to see who was visiting. "Oh, Ellen, do come in. We're watching the ocean purge itself."

"What do you mean?"

"It just dumped tons of human litter on the west coast. I'll wager that pile of trash goes from Alaska to Tierra del Fuego. And it's starting in the Gulf."

Ellen perched in the empty wooden straight chair to watch. "I was watching a movie on Turner Classics and it just ended. I had no idea of the weather. What's going on?"

Tim and Janice talked over each other in their excitement, and after Ellen raised both hands and interrupted, "Please, just one of you," Tim hushed and let Janice recount the events they had seen.

"Well, for the last century or longer, people have thrown trash into the sea, used it as a garbage dump. Some beach hotels have released sewerage into the ocean, thrown their trash into the sea at night. Same with a lot of coastal resorts. Anybody who vacationed on the beaches thought, 'What's one bottle gonna do to hurt the world?' Well, it added up."

As she paused, a voice screamed, "It's headed for *Washington*. It's a Category 5 and already with more than 200-mile winds and it's going to hit Washington. There hasn't been time for our president to evacuate."

The wide band of white with a forty-mile-wide eye swept across the image of Washington, passed westward only a few miles and vanished.

ALERT flashed across a blank screen and then to the satellite image of the Gulf. The announcer sounded more excited than concerned. "The storms in the Gulf now have winds of more than two hundred miles near the eye and are moving at more than seventy-five miles an hour. The coastal towns will be destroyed. Oh, Jesus, help them all."

The storms swallowed the Gulf coast in minutes, rushed inland and vanished. Behind lay miles of trash mingled with remains of coastal civilization.

The view returned to the studio in New York, to a man standing in shocked silence.

Another man trotted over to him and extended a sheet of paper. The visitor ran off, while the announcer read the note.

"There couldn't be more, but there is. An earthquake. A nine point four. In the mid-Atlantic. Our east coast is going to face a tsunami. It'll hit here. In New York. Oh, dear God, save me." He dropped the mike and knelt, hands clasped, palms together. And prayed.

The camera switched to a lady meteorologist. She looked directly into the camera and stated, "The satellites show that the Atlantic is pulling away from the east coast of both North and South America. From New England to Florida, people are piling into cars to flee. Roads are already jammed. Traffic cannot move. The sea is already back more than a mile—moving back at almost a mile every five minutes. We who love and live by our storms are about to die with our storms.

"Notice," she continued, "we have a tsunami forming. The ocean retreats from our coast. How far it goes back determines how high it will rise when it returns. There will be no escaping this one, just as there was no escape for those on the Pacific coast only an hour ago. I wish you well. It has been a pleasure being your weather forecaster these seven years."

The view switched to that of the satellite and showed miles of sand and more sand, and a square mile of flat stones.

"Look," Janice said. "There are the paving stones of the lost city I told you about."

The view of the paving stones lasted only a minute as the Atlantic began to move back toward the coast and rose a yard in height for every foot it traversed.

"Everybody's gonna be killed," Ellen wailed, fell to her knees and laid her head in Janice's lap.

Janice sat up, pulled Ellen up into her embrace and said, "We'll be okay, Ellen. Please. It'll be okay. Those storms can't reach us here. We might as well be a million miles away. We're going to be all right."

"I know we are," Ellen said and crawled into the bed beside Janice and clung to the older woman. "My aunt and uncle almost died in Harvey. They moved to Northern Virginia, to the coast. This will…Oh, Janice. I'm scared for them."

The tsunami rolled on, rising like a pterodactyl lifting its prey. It slammed the coast line and roared above skyscrapers, over what had been Washington, over Wall Street, and over the Statue of Liberty.

The TV screen went blank for an instant and then flashed back on from another studio.

"This is Jack Dennis reporting from Nebraska. We have lost contact with our New York studio. We will pick up the satellite relay in a moment."

The new talking head was right—the images of the tsunami reappeared. As quickly as it drowned the coast it receded as calm as a backyard pool on a windless clear day. It left behind tons of man-made trash—plastic, wood, metal, millions of bottles, used needles, broken toys—piled higher than any of the skyscrapers and the monuments it demolished.

The man in Nebraska continued. "We think this is the view of Washington, D.C. We are trying to track northward from here to where we can view New York City."

The view shifted and followed the highway of debris northward.

"Can't tell where one town stopped and another started," Janice said.

"Won't they tell us about Virginia? Oh, Janice, what about my folks? Do you think—?"

Janice pulled Ellen close into her embrace. "I fear so. I fear for everyone on the coast. It's not all their fault. The fault lies with so many people who generate so much trash. Even most of our trash doesn't get recycled either. Just dumped in landfills."

"Look at the storms," Ellen sobbed. "Are you sure they won't get here? Are we going to die too?"

Tim spoke up. "Poseidon may be mad, but his anger can't reach this far inland. "

Janice chuckled. "You mean Neptune. But yes, you are right. We won't see any of the storms here."

"Are you sure?" Ellen asked. "Look at all that rain. Can't the water back up the rivers and flood everything, the way Harvey rained on Texas?"

"Most likely not," Janice said. "At least, not for another million years, when the oceans rise to where they were a few million years ago. But we don't worry about that, now, will we? Besides, Neptune isn't mad at us, he just wants to give us back our garbage, remind us we crawled out of the ocean and that we've messed in our own bed. Even a dog doesn't mess in his own bed.

"Haven't you noticed? There is nothing of the sea in the debris. No fish, no dolphins, no whales, no shell fish, no crabs. And not even our nemesis of the seaside—no sharks. The oceans just threw back the trash we threw to them. It's Neptune's revenge."

"You mean Poseidon's," Tim said.

Hours later, while the nursing home occupants slept, the gods were pacified and the oceans also slept.

TAILHOOK REVISITED

Five years after the assaults at the Naval pilots' Tailhook gathering, anger and shame burned her every waking moment. Nightmares raged through her sleep as she relived the rapes by three of her senior officers and the horror of her no-choice-but abortion. No idea which monster was the father. No desire to rear a child by any of them.

Janice had followed the career of each one. Dickerson was at the Jacksonville Naval Air Station, Smithstone at San Diego, and Jeffery Richards, now a full commander, at Annapolis where he was teaching, of all things, ethics.

None had been disciplined while others had been refused promotion or cashiered. And finally, actions had been taken to get rid of some of the flag officers who had allowed the horror to occur. "Getting rid of," however, consisted of retirement with full benefits and another job in the government for some.

Today began a new era. She was free, at last, of the uniform. Her close friends Betty and Alice, also victims at Tailhook, had resigned in the past two weeks. Now was the time to convert their years of plans into action. Betty had been a midshipman at the Academy and knew about the Blue Moonlights, the hangout for those who wanted to hook up with a hooker or any other female.

Betty had selected the two-bedroom Craftsman cottage two miles away and had rented it by phone and with a money order in a fictitious name. The evening she arrived at the retirement home residence of the owner to pick up the key, she had padded her cheeks, turned her green eyes blue with contacts, wrapped enough padding around her middle to look forty pounds heavier, and dyed her blond hair black. The old lady had left the key with the receptionist who said the owner was delighted to rent the house and not to hesitate if everything was not in order.

Betty knew the Blue Moonlights and had drawn up a detailed plan of the inside. For three evenings, they watched the entrance from some twenty yards down the street and on the other side while they sat in the dark blue Subaru Outback Janice had rented in North Carolina a week before. Janice had turned off the inside lights before she reached Annapolis, and even while the vehicle was underway, the dashboard remained pale as a predawn sky.

The plans had been to draw straws, but Janice had insisted she be the target for their first victim. "I just need the satisfaction," she stated.

Each evening, she used dark contacts to turn her green eyes dark brown. Her brown hair was bleached blond-white. A makeup scar across her right cheek would look real in the semidarkness of the bar. Even a close-up view would fool anyone who later tried to describe her.

Each night as they waited to him to appear, their conversations often drifted back to the Tailhook Convention of 1991 and the other eighty women who had suffered as they had. "Some of those men didn't even care who they raped," Betty said. "I understand at least seven of the male pilots were also raped."

"Yes," Janice said. "My only regret with our plans is we can't include Admiral Williams for calling us all 'go-go dancers.' I would love to teach him how to go-go dance."

They laughed but with more bitterness than humor.

"At least the word will get around after we finish our plans. There'll be a lot of ex-pilots out there who will worry if they are on the list."

The third evening Janice broke the silence. "That's him. On the left."

He sauntered with the same strut they all remembered. "Let's give him a half-hour," Betty said. "Be sure he's into his liquor before you go in."

"You scared?" Alice asked.

"A little, but mostly just anticipating." Janice said. "I don't think he'll remember."

"No. No way any of them will remember any of us. They were so wrapped
up in their own egos and so sloshed. And they never faced judgment, so they never saw us. They probably don't even remember how many of us they raped. At least, after tonight, he won't rape any more navy ladies."

They fell silent again. The half-hour passed. Janice opened her door, stepped out, and tugged down the too-tight blouse that her padded breasts pushed against. She looked back. "Do I look slutty enough?"

Betty grinned, "About right. I might need to borrow that dress when we go to San Diego."

Janice nodded and grinned. "Well, girls, I'm off to bag a self-made bastard. See ya in a bit." She strode toward the door a half-block away. Street lights splashed across the darkness of the sidewalk.

She spotted the bouncer as she closed the distance.

"What does it take for a lady to gain entrance?" She smiled as she spoke.

The bouncer grinned as he gazed at her breasts. "For you, lady, there ain't no fee. You step right in."

"Thanks," she said as he opened the door. She entered the semi-darkness deeper than outside, and stood just inside to let her eyes adjust.

He saw her before she spotted him, and as she headed to the bar, he intercepted her.

"Well, hello there, beautiful. Where've you been hiding all this time?"

If his eyes could touch, she would have felt them from breasts to crotch and back up.

"Oh, I just got to town. I'm new here and looking for some sailor-style fun."

"You're in the right place to start with, the wrong place for the rest of the night."

She felt her jaw begin to tighten with anger and had to concentrate to relax and counter his banter.

"Is that a proposition?" She forced herself to meet his gaze, to look at the face that haunted her for four years. She reminded herself this is the night, this is *IT*.

"Only if you want it to be."

"Well, let me have a look at the available studs. You don't look like much."

His eyes narrowed. "Oh, you think not, huh?"

She shrugged. "Well, you don't give me a hard on. Do I give you one, junior?"

She grinned and patted his crotch. "Oh, how about that."

She turned away and headed to the bar.

He grabbed her arm. "Don't you walk away from me, young lady. Not after that enticement."

"And don't you get bossy, buddy." She looked down at his hand.

He released her arm. "Sorry. But you've gotten to me. What can I do to make amends? Maybe supper and dancing?"

She propped her right elbow on her left arm crossed over her belly and tapped a finger against her lower lip. "Well, let me ponder a moment." The noise of the bar swirled around them. She pointed her right forefinger at him, "Tell you what. I've had supper. And I know what kind of dancing you have in mind. I have the perfect site for dancing at home. You come to my place in, say a half-hour? Give me a chance to ahhh, to get the dance floor polished just right. And we'll see if you can hold that." She pointed to his crotch.

"Give me the address. I'll wait with bated breath."

"Don't hurry. I want to surprise you. I won't open the door until," she looked at her watch, "11:15. Even if you try to knock it down. So don't knock. Just walk in."

She pulled an index card from between her breasts and handed it to him. He put it to his nose and sniffed. "Nice." He read the address, grinned, looked at his watch, and said, "Wait for me. I'll be there."

"Eleven-fifteen is when I'll unlock the door." She turned and strode out the door. The bouncer said, "Leaving already? The night's young."

"So it is. But I'm headed out. See you next time."

"Don't be a stranger."

"I won't." *Like hell. This is the last time I'll be in Annapolis. Next stop will be Jacksonville and then San Diego. After that, home to Iowa and a peaceful life.*

At 11:15 sharp, he pushed open the door and stood facing darkness and his own silhouette outlined by the street light.

"Come on in," she whispered the invitation. "And close the door."

He stepped inside and pushed the door to.

Someone moved behind him and in the darkness he heard a lock click. Footsteps circled him.

Lights came on. Three people greeted him. All were clad in white jumpsuits with the Tailhook Association badge on the left breast.

Each wore surgical gloves and dust masks. Until one spoke, he could not even determine their sex. In the middle, Janice held a Glock 42 in her right hand. Her eyes narrowed to slits. The hand holding the weapon did not move.

"Come on in, Jeffery Richards. Welcome to Tailhook Revisited."

"What's going on? Who are you? Who are any of you?"

"We're three of those who had the displeasure of your *amorous* activities at the Tailhook Symposium back in '91."

"What the hell are you talking about? That situation's been investigated and is over with."

"See?" Alice said. "I told you he wouldn't remember. None of them will remember any of the women."

"I'm leaving," he said and turned toward the door. Alice waved the key. "I don't think so. We're going to have a party, a Tailhook party. And you're the guest of honor."

She walked to the coffee table and lifted a glass of a brown liquid in ice. "Here's to you and fun and games, Tailhook style." She offered him the glass. "Drink up."

"What is that? Poison?"

"No, just your favorite. We call it Tailhook bourbon on the rocks. Taste it."

He took the glass and sniffed.

"Oh, don't be such a sissy. Drink it down. Or do you want some encouragement?"

Janice pointed the pistol to his face and Betty showed him a Taser. "Better to drink than suffer the 'or else'."

His hand trembled as he raised the glass. He hesitated as the glass touched his lips and lowered it.

"No, no. Drink."

He drank.

Moments later, he began to slump. "What did you put in that?"

"Same thing you put in the ladies' drinks at Tailhook, just so you could have some fun. Now it's our time to have the fun."

He collapsed onto the floor.

Janice placed the pistol on the coffee table, reached down and pulled on his left arm. "I got one arm. Let's get him to the kitchen."

Alice grabbed the other arm and Betty grabbed his feet. In the kitchen, they lifted him onto a metal-top table. In minutes they had him naked. Betty, who had castrated hogs on the family farm while in her teens, swabbed him down with Betadine and performed the surgery. They didn't bother with a bandage but slid on a pair of Depends before they pulled on his boxer shorts and slacks.

He began to awaken and tottered a bit as they dragged him to his Jaguar and placed him in the passenger seat. They hurried to load their gear into the Outback. No need to swab off fingerprints in the house—they had touched nothing without their surgical gloves.

Still in the jumpsuit and gloves, Alice scrambled behind the wheel of the Jag and drove the vehicle to within four blocks of the Blue Moonlights and parked by a fire hydrant.

The others followed in the SUV and helped Alice slid him into the driver's seat. She leaned his head against the steering wheel. They scurried into the Subaru and left Maryland.

Next stop, Naval Air Station, Jacksonville.

An hour later, he woke up to the sound of someone knocking on his window.

"Hey, mister, let down your window. You drunk? Howcome you're parked at the fire hydrant?"

He shook his head and felt pain in his crotch. He looked down and something to his right caught his attention—a Ziploc bag containing bloody objects and a piece of paper with large boldfaced computer print.

Rocky Mountain oysters are said to be good roasted. Maybe you should try Tailhook oysters.

He screamed. The cop busted the window with his Billy club and hauled the babbling, drunk sailor to jail.

THREE STRANGERS

Amy opened her backdoor to go to the barn. Her redbone hound Jasper dashed ahead of her into the fog.

The stink of a distant fire grated at her nose as she stepped outside. *Something's burning somewhere. Doesn't smell like just woods though.*

When she slid the barn door open, Jasper dashed to the first stall and yipped. The stallion nodded his head and whickered back. She turned the three horses into the pasture so she could muck the stalls. Jasper flopped down in the unused stall for his after-breakfast nap while she worked.

Her annoyance at conversations yesterday returned. Farmers had gossiped at the feed store about a family of wetbacks who moved into the Johnson farm. "You be careful out there by yourself. You know them illegals are nothing but rapists and thieves and killers."

Another had said, "Thank God they don't have a litter of children or we'd have them in school and have to teach them English."

She wanted to scream at him. His family had migrated here from Germany after the First World War. She wondered if his grandfather had automatically spoken perfect English when he stepped off the boat. She shook her head at her thoughts.

Humanity was about as dense as the fog.

Outside, one of the horses snorted. Jasper rose, came to her side and growled as he looked toward the open door.

Sunlight now streamed through the fog. Three figures stood at the door.

Jasper growled again, lowered his body into a crouch and began to stalk the strangers.

Hispanics. Illegals.

"You men should move along," she said. "I don't want any problems with Border Patrol."

"Please Ma'am, don't let the dog get us."

Oh dear Gussie, I'm as bad as the rest of town. They aren't killers. They're hurt. "No, Jasper, here boy. Sit."

The dog retreated to her side and sat.

The face of the man in the middle was bruised, his left eye swollen closed. He draped an arm over the shoulder of the thinnest man she had ever seen. The injured man stood on one foot. The other leg was tied to a stick and held up, bent at the knee. The third man carried a green oak limb as a walking stick and had the injured man's other arm over his shoulder.

The thin man spoke in Southern-accented English. "Please, Ma'am. They tried to kill him with their fists and a baseball bat. They killed our mother. They burned our house. We mean no harm. They hate us because we are Hispanic, but we are American. We are brothers, born here. As were our parents."

Amy shook her head as if to shake off a fly. "What? Who did this? Who are you?"

"We bought the old Johnson house and farm. Two weeks ago. We don't know who they are. They came up on us last night while we were making repairs on the barn. We saw their sheets and hoods and ran, but they caught up with Roberto here and almost killed him. Then they went into our house and killed our mother and burned down the house. We have nowhere to hide. Please. May we hide in your barn tonight? We can finish the work here. Do any job you have if you can hide us overnight. Then we will be gone."

They had walked fourteen miles cross-country in the dark.

She dropped the pitchfork and walked over to Roberto. One look at his face and she knew his nose was broken. Maybe his jaw also.

"Come on to the house. I'm going to call a friend. He's a doctor and he'll tend to Roberto. He has to have a doctor."

"We have nothing now, Ma'am. We can't pay for a doctor now, with the house and everything else gone."

"Don't worry, he's a friend. And the grandson of immigrants. He'll understand and help you."

A half hour later, Dr. Richards arrived with his medical kit. Amy met him at the door.

"The three of them just showed up. One is in bad shape. The Ku Klux almost killed him. Burned their home and killed their mother inside the house."

"Yeah. I heard rumors of an illegal family moving into the old Johnson house."

"They say they're citizens."

"Yeah? I think most of them try to claim citizenship. They never can prove it. Let me see what I can do for him anyway."

They walked into the living room. "Roberto, this is my friend Dr. Jerry Richards. I told you about him. Jerry, this is Roberto with the broken leg and his brothers, William and Alberto."

He examined Roberto, said he needed to x-ray the leg and the face, but Roberto said he couldn't dare go to the hospital. He was frightened of whoever those men were.

Richards inspected Roberto's jaw and declared it not broken. He set the nose and turned to Amy. "I need him to lie down to set the leg."

"Let's get him into the bedroom," she said.

"You got to be kidding," Richards said.

"No, Jerry. That's the best place. It's my grandpa's old four-poster and it's tall enough you won't have to bend over to work on the leg."

She went to the kitchen pantry and removed an oilcloth table cover. "Come on. He can lie on this instead of bleeding on grandma's knitted spread."

Roberto's brothers carried him into the bedroom and settled him on the bed, close enough to the foot and the edge for Richards to work on the leg.

He cut away the make-shift splint and the man's overalls' leg. The flesh had turned black and swollen. "I really need him in the hospital," Richards said.

"No hospital," Roberto said. "Those men would hear I was there. I don't want to die—I came close enough today."

"Okay," Richards said. Roberto gritted his teeth and moaned but did not cry out as Richards manipulated the bones.

"Good thing you told me when you called that he had a broken leg. Let me get the splint from the car. Be right back."

A half-hour later, he had the splint in place and offered Roberto pain pills.

"What are these little pills?" Roberto asked.

"Oxycodone," Richards said.

"Oh, no, doctor. I'll just take Tylenol. I don't want anything that strong. Besides, we have to go so Miss Amy will not have trouble."

"No one knows you are here," Amy said. "You can't just go walking away with nowhere to go. Stay here until you can figure out what to do."

The thin brother spoke up. "No, Miss Amy. We can't put you in danger. And we have no money to pay you for your help."

"But you have no plans. No home to go back to. Stay here a few days. Don't worry about paying me rent. You two can help me a little. We'll work it out." She smiled. "I promise, I won't treat you as if you're slave labor. I do need some help."

Richards said, "Well, I'll check back tomorrow after office hours to see how you're doing. I am going to insist that you take these pills." He handed Roberto a packet. "Two now, and one a day until they run out. They're antibiotics and will keep you from getting infected."

He started to leave, stopped at the bedroom door, and said, "One of you fellas come out to the car. I have crutches you can bring in."

When the thin brother returned with the crutches, Roberto sat up and began to ease off the bed. "I cannot stay in your bed, Miss Amy. I can lie on the floor."

"Not on the floor. I have two other rooms. The bed in one is lower, so you can get in and out easier."

She showed the men the two guest rooms, which shared a bath. She told them to clean up, there were towels aplenty in the guest bath.

"I have clothes that won't fit well, but there are work pants and shirts in the closet from when my brother stayed here last summer. Use whatever you need. Now, I need to get your names, your parents' names and where you were born. I'm going to get your birth certificates and clear all this up with the sheriff."

Roberto said, "That's too much for you to do, Miss Amy."

"No, it's not."

They provided the information and she went to her computer. They had been born in Tickleboro, slightly more than one hundred miles away to the north. She knew Deputy Hicks there and called him.

After she and Deputy Hicks laughed again at the episode of Junior and the fake bass that had stirred up national attention that summer, she told him what she needed. "Send me copies of each certificate by overnight mail. I've got to put a stop to what's going on over here."

He agreed.

Two hours later, he called to say the copies were in the mail, registered and overnight expressed to her and also to the local sheriff.

Sheriff Fuller reached her house before her registered letter. He had his copies and greeted her with, "What's this all about?"

"The KKK got ahold of this family a couple of days ago. Insisted they were illegal and killed their mother and almost killed one of the brothers. They are here. I'm afraid to let them leave. I have no idea who the KKK people are around here. I thought they had dissolved."

"No, they haven't dissolved. Now they are after anyone they think shouldn't be here. I heard they got after some Muslims down south of here last week. Don't you ever watch the news? It's been all over television."

"I reached the point during the election campaigns that I couldn't watch any news. I just watch nature programs now."

He smiled. "I don't blame you. Let me see if I can get the word out about your guys being citizens and maybe, just maybe, the white-sheeted ones will listen to reason. But I'll have to see about the murder of the mother and the arson."

"Let's hope something can be done. Please don't let anyone know they are here."

"I'll keep it quiet." He left.

The four of them had just finished supper and darkness had fallen when shouts outside warned them.

Amy went to the hall closet, pulled out her .12 gauge pump Remington, removed the plug, shoved four shells into the magazine, and walked to the front door. Some men in white sheets were digging a hole for the cross when she opened the door.

She pumped the shotgun. The voices quieted.

"Now, now, Miss Amy. You put that there gun down."

"I don't think so, Jerry. You're sworn to keep your mouth shut. Now get a move on. Fill that hole back up, put that damn cross back on your truck and you get off my land. You come back here, you won't be driving away. You'll leave in a body bag. Do I make myself clear?"

"You're harboring some illegal wetbacks."

"Jerry, they are as legal as you. You're second generation Polish, aren't you? Don't you think it's time you got burned out and your immigrant mama burned up in the house?"

"What're you talking about?"

"You burned up their mama. You know damned well you killed her. Supposing it had been your mama? These friends of yours should put the match to your house. You're as much an illegal as these men are. They were all born up the road in Tickleboro."

"No."

"Oh, yeah. Now get the hell off my land and don't come back. I don't want to even see your immigrant face in town ever again. You understand what I mean, Jerry? You have no rights that these men don't have too. You understand me? And you better be prepared cause Sheriff Fuller's gonna come calling on you."

A voice from the darkness called, "You better be getting out of town, Jerry. You messed up. You damned them for being what you are, you bastard. Look what you done got us to do cause we been damn stupid enough to follow the likes of you."

Another voice called. "Amy, we can't bring their mama back, but we for sure can do something about fixing their house."

The men vanished into the shadows.

Amy wondered what their town would do without a doctor.

GERALD RIVERS RADIO/TV INTERVIEW
with
TICKLEBORO JAIL FUGITIVE

Camera focuses on Rivers' face. He holds a microphone with the Tickleboro radio station logo WTKL.

"This is Gerald Rivers, reporting from Georgia, at the Tickleboro jail, where I will interview Willie Jackson live, about the two prisoners who escaped from a transfer bus two months ago and have not been caught. In spite of the $150,000 reward.

"We are being broadcast simultaneously on national radio and on the local Tickleboro TV station. I understand the local deputies are authorized to listen in on their car radios while on patrol."

Camera pans to Willie, who wears an orange jump suit and sits at a table with his hands not cuffed but resting on the table. He is clean shaven; his hair cut is recent.

"Willie, I must tell our listening audience about the agreement between you and me, the reason you have agreed to give this interview. Is this okay with you?"

Willie nods. Camera focuses on Rivers.

"Okay, Willie, you indicate it is okay with you. For you out there watching or listening, Willie agreed to tell us everything he saw the day of the great escape. There was a camera aboard the transport vehicle, but the escapees destroyed it so the images were lost. None of the other prisoners who were on the bus would talk to us. In fact, all others have refused to talk to law enforcement. But Willie agreed since his term will be up in another two weeks and we have offered him a rather hefty fee. Plus, this interview, although it is shown live, is also being recorded for the Tickleboro district attorney's office for future use. And the district attorney has promised not to send him back to the state prison but to let him finish his sentence here, in the Tickleboro jail, where he'll be safe."

He turns from the camera to look at Willie.

"You were on the prisoner transfer bus on June 21, weren't you?"

"Yes, Sir."

"Tell us what happened that day. Begin with where you were sitting and where others were located."

"Yes, Sir. Well, I was sitting on the left-hand front seat. It's a bench, and I was on the side next to the aisle. Boo and Juice were across the aisle, in the front seat next to the door. I couldn't hear all they said to each other, but I could see what-all they was doing. Boo pulled a hair pin out of his hair and used it to unlock they hand cuffs."

"He used a hair pin?"

"Yes, Sir. The guards never look at a man's hair to see what he's got hidden there. They check our pockets and even look to see what we might have in our shoes, but I ain't never seed a guard look in anybody's hair. And Boo has got a whole heap of hair. He could of hid a shank there if it weren't a long one."

"I understand it is routine to do a body search. A strip search."

"I thought so too. But they didn't."

"So Boo unlocked the handcuffs with a bobby pin he hid in his hair. Did he offer to free anybody else?"

Willie shakes his head.

"Willie, please answer out loud. We are on the radio as well as on the TV camera. The radio listeners need to hear your answers."

"Yes, Sir. I mean, no-Sir, he didn't say nothing to anybody about letting us go too. If he done offered to unlock me, I would of said 'no' cause I get out in two more weeks. I don't want to add any more time by trying to run. Escaping don't help in the long run, Sir. You best off to do your time."

"Then what did he do? How did he get beyond the grill work into the front compartment?"

"It weren't locked. There was a lock hanging on the other side, but it weren't locked. It was almost like they wanted them two to get away."

"Not locked? Why wasn't it locked? Isn't it always locked?"

"Lots of times they don't bother. See, any of the lifers and they buddies, they puts on the front so the guards can watch them. But all of us, they handcuff two of us together and one of us's hand to the rail on the seat. They don't see need to lock the lock on the grill door. Everybody at the jail knows the lock is just hanging there and mostly ain't locked."

"And what did the guards do when Boo unlocked the cuffs?"

"Didn't neither one of the guards look back. One of 'em was leaned back against the wall. Dead asleep and snoring loud enough he wasn't hearing anything going on back where we was. Other one what was driving, he never looked once in the mirror or even at the other guard."

He paused and looked over at the camera and the man behind it. He looked back at Rivers who said, "The guards didn't know they were loose?"

"No, Sir. Boo and Juice just got up and opened the grill door and walked in the front of the bus." *He looked down at his hands, twisted in his lap. His eyebrows lifted and he sighed.*

"You said the lock was hanging on the door. Was it hooked in the hasp?"

"Yes, Sir. They always hang it there. Boo, he just took out his toothbrush—"

"Toothbrush? He had his toothbrush in his pocket?"

"He shore enough did. Like I said the guards, they didn't really search us before we got on the bus. Boo, he just pulled out his toothbrush and stuck it through the grill and under the lock and just lifted it up. He held it up like that and opened the grill door and he and Juice walked into the front."

"So they just walked in on the guards. One asleep and the other with his mind only on the road. Go on. Then what happened?"

"Well, Sir, it was like I said. One of them was sleeping. They guns and they vests was laid out on the extra seat where another guard would have been. Juice jest reached over, picked up one of them guns, and shot the sleeping guard four times right in the chest where his vest would-a been."

"You mean to say the guards just laid their guns on the extra seat? Neither one of them had them buckled on like they were supposed to wear them?"

"Yes, Sir, that be right. All us at the jail hear talk the guards don't like to wear them vests cause they so hot. And it was shore hot that day. We was sweating something fierce in the bus."

"But their guns. They should have had them strapped on. If they just laid them down in reach of the grill doorway—" *Rivers voice faded.*

"Yes Sir, that's what they say at the jail. The guards don't like them gun belts. The one sleeping couldn't get easy with it strapped on, I reckon. And a gun belt with that there Billy club and stuff would be in the way for the driver. So they never wear 'em in the bus, I hear tell."

"So was it Boo or Juice who killed Mr. Eckerds?"

"It was Juice. He shot and he laughed and turned around and grinned at Boo and then waved at us in the back."

"What did the driver do? Didn't he try to stop them?"

"Well, Sir, the driver stopped the bus and looked back to see what all happened. Boo pointed the other gun at him, what he had picked up from the extra seat too. And Boo told him to open up the door so they could get out. The driver, he said he weren't supposed to open up the door. Boo said, 'Too bad,' and shot him right there where-at he sat. Shot him six times. Then he opened up the door hisself."

He paused again, as if waiting for Rivers to ask another question. He looked down at his hands which he had begun to twist into each other as if worried over what might happen to him because he was telling the truth instead of saying nothing or even lying like he knew the other prisoners had when interviewed by the police. He knew they had said they didn't see anything.

He looked up at the camera and at the mirror. He knew local officers were behind there, watching. And who knew who else was there too. All he wanted was to get this over with and get free in a few days.

"What's the matter, Willie?"

"I just be scared. I shore don't want to go back to the jailhouse. Even if they never catch Juice and Boo, I ain't gonna be alive long after this here. If they get cotched or not."

"We have already arranged it so you don't go back to the state prison. You will be saying here, in the Tickleboro jail, for the rest of your sentence."

"That what you say, Sir, but everybody know it don't matter whereat you in jail. Word gets out you talk about stuff, you get kilt."

"We'll do all we can to protect you, Willie. Besides, I have been authorized to tell you, because of your cooperation, the federal government also wants to thank you for your help. You'll get to be a free man and the federal government will even give you a new identity to help protect you. It'll help you get an education or training to do any kind of work you want, all for helping put Boo and Juice away. So, please, go on. What happened next?"

He shrugged. "They got out-a the bus onto the road and took the extra clips with them. They musta had at least a hundred bullets and them two fancy pistols. Wasn't no way, I figured, they'd ever get caught and be alive.

"They wasn't out on the road long afore a car come along. The green one everybody looked for all that day. The man stopped and they pointed the pistols at him and I was for sure they was gonna kill him too, but they didn't. He got out and they took the car and left.

"Hit was another hour afore the next car come along. We was about to sweat to death inside that there bus. We couldn't get out seeing as how we all was handcuffed to the seats. Anyhow, Dexter—he was in for burglary same as me—he said for us to sit still. If we tried to get loose and get out of the bus, he said, we could be called guilty of killing the guards too. So we sat.

"It was powerful hot. I ain't sweated that much pitching hay when it was brinjin hot in July on the farm whereabouts I was raised up."

"No one opened a window or anything?"

"No, Sir. Them windows, they was locked down. Don't none of them open up. We didn't have no water and nowhere to piss neither. It was damn hot. Even when that other car come along and the first white man waves him down and he stopped cause he saw something was bad, we didn't move. Hit was a lot longer afore Mr. Sheriff Bates let us get off and get in the shade. He had his deputies bring us all a bottle of water too and said we could piss in the bushes alongside the road." *He smiles.* "Didn't nobody have to piss, howsomever. We done sweated out all our piss.

"And Mr. Sheriff Bates, he asked us all about what happened before the new bus come along to take us on to our new jail. But nobody said nothing. They scared to speak, same as me."

"Thank you, Willie. That's all I have for you today."

The camera focuses on a deputy standing against the wall by the door.

"Deputy Wilson, please take Willie to the safety of your local jail here."

Wilson strides to the table and takes Willie by the arm.

"Come along, Willie."

Willie rises and is led to the door. The camera focuses on Rivers.

"Well, folks, Willie has answered some of the questions we all had. How did the prisoners unlock their handcuffs? How did they get through the protective door from the bus to the guards? How did they overpower the guards?"

From the hallway comes the sound of a body slammed against the wall and loud voices.

"I'll kill you no matter where you are, you yellow-bellied money sucker! You talk to damn much. I heard every damn word you said on the radio."

"No, Willie! Put it down!"

"You ain't gone let 'im kill me. I got money coming fer what all I said."

Gunfire.

Rivers stands mute. The camera focuses on the doorway. Rivers opens the door.

Boo stands looking down. A deputy holds a smoking pistol. Two legs clad in jail-house orange show on the floor. Deputy Wilson looks at the camera and says, "Willie grabbed my gun. He was going to shoot Boo. Joe had to shoot him. He's dead."

Rivers turned to the camera. "Well, there you have it. The one witness who would help convict Boo tries to kill him and instead gets himself shot to death by a deputy in the very same jail where we promised him safety. This is Gerald Rivers saying goodnight from the Tickleboro jail."

The screen fades to black.

SARAH

Ben knew he should not have tried to find the stray horse with a storm coming on. Remembering the mare that tore through the fence in a similar storm only last year, he gritted his teeth. Heavy drops began to pelt his back, and he ran, his head ducked, his youthful legs not feeling the strain of the climb up the rocky ridge to the limestone cave.

Just sixty yards up the ridge, the cave offered shelter a mile closer than the house. Lightning slashed a pine off to his left, and he increased his speed. He could not only get out of the rain but he could build a fire and dry off. His leather jacket and heavy-duty canvas pants deflected thorns as he pushed through the last of the thickets. He stepped into the cave entrance.

Inside, he turned to look back. A multi-branched flash lit up the valley below and turned the deluge to silver.

He wiped rain off his face, gaunt in spite of his twenty-four years. Red half-moons hung beneath his eyes, and white streaked his black hair. He shivered and ran calloused hands through his hair to push out water.

With a sigh, he backed into the dimness.

Somewhere over to his left lay wood he had piled up when he and Sarah planned to explore the cave, the day before that storm last year, when she had looked for another stray horse and vanished. The pain of loss and its mystery gripped him.

He had gone to town that day, to the feed store, and come home to find a note—the last words he had from her. The mare Marietta, expecting a foal, had kicked down the half-door of her stall, jumped the paddock fence and gone off to who-knows-where.

Marietta had come home two days later, her foal trotting behind her. But Sarah had not come home. Every man and half the women in the county had helped search for her for three days.

The sheriff two counties away reported a woman's body floating down a river more than twenty miles away—a river that did not pass through their land or even through the county.

He shook his head as if to throw remembering from his mind, reached for a match in his pocket, struck it, and in the faint light looked for his woodpile. Before the flame reached his fingers, he stepped across the small chamber toward to wood. Match light danced off the stalactites.

Only a pile of ashes and a few sticks remained. Darkness fell as he dropped the match.

Sarah. She must have come here too, that day. If only he had thought about the cave then. But there was no other sign she had been here. Just ashes and missing wood.

"No," he shouted, gripped the sides of his head and rocked on his feet.

"No," he whispered. His voice echoed from all directions.

He sank onto the damp floor, his back to the wall. Another lightning strike lit the chamber and drew his eyes back to the few remaining sticks of wood.

Oh, Sarah, if only. If only I had thought. But if you here, how in God's own hell did you get into the river twenty miles away?

He pulled out his pocket knife—the one Sarah had given him—picked up the largest stick and began to whittle kindling. In a few minutes he had a pile of shavings on the floor. Another match set them afire, and he carefully laid most of the sticks on the tiny flame and built up the blaze. The storm's violence drowned the fire's friendly crackle.

He glanced about the chamber. Long spikes clung to the ceiling and in the firelight gleamed like icicle swords. The suggestion made him shiver, and he moved closer to his fire. His shadow leaped along the wall like a guardian of the cavern.

In spite of knowing he was alone, he felt chill-like fingers creep down his back. He squinted as he searched for someone in the darkness behind him.

Only his shadow moved, a darker image dancing against the distant wall. Nothing but the fire's voices and the storm broke the silence.

He leaned against the cold limestone, grateful for the leather jacket that kept away the seeping dampness. But his mind kept looking back into that yesterday, when he had wanted to die himself. When he had failed to think of the cave as a shelter for Sarah.

He wept. His body shook. His chest felt raw and his belly ached with pain. He lay down, curled into himself.

The flames flickered, and Ben's sobs softened. He slept.

Ben stirred. The storm had ended. He opened his eyes to see a faint red beneath the ashes and to hear the silence of a storm ended. He sat up, his back to the quiet of the outside world. He faced the back of the cavern and entrance to the tunnel they had never explored.

From the depths of the cavern floated the white-clad figure of a girl, unsmiling, grave, solemn.

"No—it can't be!" he whispered and scrambled to his feet.

"Sarah!" he said, then, more softly, "Sarah?" His own voice whispered back "Sarah? Sarah?" until the name faded into nothingness. He stepped toward her.

The figure backed away. Gestured.

"Come."

The word and the gesture drew him. He stumbled forward and followed the form into the single narrow passage where darkness intensified and silence deepened. Around bends and past other tunnels, he followed. His stumbling became a steady stride.

The walls shimmered as if fire danced inside the ice and the darkness brightened to twilight. Silence gave way to the drip of water from the spires overhead, and he began to slip on the wetness.

Ben had to reach to the tunnel walls to keep his balance. A distant roar swallowed the sounds of seeping water and began to pound his head as it echoed from the walls.

The apparition paused.

"Sarah? I'm coming."

She vanished.

He stopped, puzzled. He stepped forward, felt emptiness below his toe, and jumped back. Leaning over, he looked down into a gulch.

A river boiled through the rocks and rushed along the chasm it had cut in the limestone some fifty feet below. She stood on one of the rocks.

"Come," she whispered, her voice soft and gentle in the roar of the river.

He reached out, stepped forward, and plunged down—down—down until he was coughing and sputtering in water.

Ben sat up and wiped water from his face, silently fussing at himself for going to sleep, falling face downward in a puddle the storm left behind, and letting his fire die down.

He remembered dreaming but could not summon the dream back to his awake mind.

He glanced around the cavern. The coals could not light the vast room, could not keep back the heavy, black shadows thrown by the rising moon's light through the cave entrance.

"Oh, my God!" he muttered.

Across the chamber, merging with the shadows, stood Sarah, in white, her arms outstretched.

"Come," she whispered.

BROKEN BONES

The father watched his son pick berries and decided the boy was too sissy. What boy picked berries and laughed with other children—all girls and a few boys not even old enough for first grade. He walked up to his son, grabbed the bucket, swung it and scattered the berries into the brush. He dropped the bucket and stomped it twice.

"No, Pa," the boy cried.

"Don't you *No Pa* me." He kicked the boy in the shin, turned and walked away.

The boy crumpled and gripped his leg just above where the steel toe hit. Blood seeped from the gash. He rocked with pain and fought the need to cry. Tears flowed but he swallowed the sound. At thirteen, he had to be a man. He wasn't about to call for one of the girls, even one of the older girls, to help him. The other children continued to pick berries. Mama had promised him a blackberry pie if he was willing to bring home some berries. Bushes heavy with berries lined the fence row and everybody was out for berries that afternoon. He looked at what was left of his bucket. It wouldn't even hold a handful of berries.

He gathered himself and managed to stand. His leg throbbed. He tried to walk, but the pain was too intense for him to put weight on that leg. He hopped a few steps.

A younger boy came over and asked him if he could help. Jake looked at the child. He had a bucket half filled with berries and reached up to Jake and said, "You can have some of my berries."

"No, Sammy, I can't take your berries. You see that stick over there?" He pointed to a fallen hickory limb. Sammy nodded. "Would you bring it here to me?"

Sammy trotted over, picked up the stick which was longer than he was tall, and carried it to Jake.

Jake thanked him and tested the stick. It bent but was still green and did not break. One end forked. He hopped to a nearby log. He knew he would get covered up with redbugs but what else could he do. He perched on the log.

Jake reached into his overalls pocket and pulled out a folding Buck knife. He began to whittle on the stick to cut off a length about three feet. Sammy sat by him and watched.

"Whatcha doing?" he asked.

"I'm gonna fix my leg so I can walk better. You got a handkerchief?"

Sammy dug into his pocket and removed a soiled handkerchief. Jake did not hesitate but reached for it. He fashioned a splint and used his and Sammy's handkerchiefs to strap the stick onto his leg and cover the gash. *At least the bleeding's stopped.*

He stood. The rest of the hickory stick was long enough for him to lean on the fork and use for a crutch. He headed home. It would be a long hobble.

He limped into the front yard and passed his father who lay sprawled out and asleep at the base of the oak that shaded their home. "Passed out drunk again," Jake muttered. He went inside.

His mother called, "That you, son?"

"Yes, Mama."

"You bringing me some berries for your pie?"

"No, Mama. I don't got no berries."

He made it to the room he shared with two younger brothers and dropped onto the bed beside the sleeping four-year-old.

His mama came into the room. "Howcome you didn't get any berries?"

Jake thought for a moment and told the truth for the first time. "Pa didn't think a boy ought to be picking berries. He flung mine away."

"Howcome you got that-there stick? Oh, what happened to your leg?"

"Mama, he kicked me. It hurts so bad I was scared to just walk home on it."

She looked at the leg. A knot rising on his shin made the leg look bent. The bruise had begun to turn black and to slide down his leg. "Your pa give you that-there pone? I don't believe you."

"Ma, it ain't the first time. I ain't taking no more."

"What do you mean, it ain't the first time?"

"He busted my arm last year."

"You said you fell off the porch."

"He said if I told you he'd break the other arm. So I ain't told you. But I ain't taking it no more."

"I'll get some turpentine and swab that-there pone. The skin don't have to be broke open for it to help take the sore out."

She was back in a moment with one of Pa's sleeveless tee shirts. She poured some turpentine onto the rag and laid it over the knot still rising on his leg.

They heard Pa stumbling into the house. Ma left the room and a moment later Jake heard her accusing Pa of breaking his leg.

"He got what he deserved. He got no truck with picking berries like a damn girl. I'll make a man of him if I have to kill him."

"He's just a boy!"

No words. The sound of fist on flesh and a house-shaking thump as Ma hit the floor.

Jake got to his feet and looked around the room. Nothing but the self-made cane he used to walk. He stumbled into the hall and saw Ma lying on the floor, her face swelling. Pa wasn't there.

Noises in the kitchen. Jake hobbled in.

Pa looked up from where he was exploring the Frigidaire for another beer.

"Whatcha doing leaning on that there stick like you hurt or something?" Pa asked.

Jake grinned. "You just about broke my leg, Pa. I just need some help to walk. You finding any beer in there?"

"Yeah." He smiled. "You want one? You man enough to have a beer with your pa?"

Jake nodded. "Yeah, Pa. I can take this here busted leg, I can shore use a beer."

Pa grabbed two beers and handed one to his son. Jake watched how Pa pulled the tab to open the beer and opened his own.

Pa drank his down without lowering the can. "You do that, boy?"

"Not yet, Pa. Give me a couple of days to learn, and I will."

Pa reached over for Jake's beer, pulled it from the child's hand and stumbled down the hall and outside again.

Jake followed to the front door and watched. Pa was soon leaning up against the tree and snoozing.

Ma was no longer in the front hallway. Blood on the floor and smeared on the wall caught Jake's attention. He went to find Ma.

She lay on her back on the bed, on top of the quilt she had worked on for several years. Blood stained it.

"Ma? Are you okay?"

"Oh, Jake, honey. Are you okay? How's the leg?"

"It hurts. I'm gonna kill him, Ma. He got no right to be hitting you."

"No, son, you can't. We'll leave. You and me and the two other boys."

"Where we gonna go, Ma? You ain't got no kin around here excepting Uncle Grant. You think we can live with him and Miss Ellie? She don't cater to me none."

"We'll figure it out. Go lie down. I'll call Grant to come fix your leg."

"Yessum," Jake muttered. But instead of going to his room, he hobbled to the front porch, sat on the floor at the steps and bounced down the stairs on his butt. He used the railing to pull himself up and limped over to his father.

Flat on his back, Pa snored as he slept off his drunk.

Jake raised his walking stick and aimed the fork at his father's face. As he swung, his balance wavered and he slammed one end into his father's throat.

Pa never woke up.

SUNDAY AFTERNOON GOLF

"Dad, I'd like to play golf with you this afternoon," Buddy said as the three sat down to the family's standard Sunday after-church dinner of roast beef.

Carl's hand stopped in midair for a fraction and then he filled his mouth with the bite of steak, chewed, and swallowed.

"Well, Dad? May I join you today?"

"We have a regular foursome on Sundays now. I'll take off work tomorrow and we can go. Or next Saturday. I just can't break up the foursome. We've been together for, oh, I don't know. About three years." He smiled at his wife. "I would love to have someone in the family play golf with me."

"Sweetheart, I thought Bob had to bring along his sister-in-law to make up the four, didn't he?" Andrea said. "Why not take Buddy?"

"Oh. Yes, but she's not just an extra. She's one hell of a golfer. Beats us all the time. Makes us all play better. I just can't ask her to drop out. The others would be upset."

"Dad, why doesn't her husband play golf?"

"Vernon?" Carl chuckled. "I think he's too absorbed in himself to do anything but paint. He's an artist. In fact, he's opening an art show next week."

"Is his work any account?"

"Well, since some of his paintings bring thousands, a lot of people must think so." He smiled. "Beverly sure brags on his work."

Andrea frowned. Something about the way Carl looked when he spoke of Beverly. But the look disappeared as he turned his attention back to his thick slice of rare beef and began to cut it into small pieces. Not like him. He usually just cut off the next bite, royalty style.

Buddy sighed. "Okay, Dad. Let's plan on Saturday."

Carl turned the conversation to Buddy's college classes. After dinner, he was into his golf clothes and gone before Andrea had the dishwasher filled.

He returned while she was in the den reading one of Faye Kellerman's suspense novels.

"How'd you do?" she called. "Break eighty today?"

He laughed. "I wish. I don't seem to get any better."

"Don still beating you?"

"Every week. I'm going to shower."

"That Beverly whupping you too?"

He replied over his shoulder. "Yeah. I think I'm going to try to play more and get better." He headed for their master suite.

She sighed. He'd have thrown his clothes on the floor. *Might as well go tend to them now. Why can't men learn to put their dirties in the hamper?*

Sure enough, everything was piled on the floor. She lifted his trousers, removed his wallet and car and house keys, and checked other pockets. A piece of paper in the left-hand pocket. She pulled it out and un-crumbled it. Receipt. *Where...? What? Best Western? Today?*

She almost collapsed as she sank on the edge of the bed. *He's having an affair. My god. After twenty years I can't believe he's that stupid, to let me catch him like this.*

She was still sitting on the bed, the receipt in hand, when, clad only in a towel, he walked in from the shower. He paused when he saw her.

She looked up. "The Best Western, Carl?"

He blushed, clamped his teeth and tilted his head. "Yeah, well, I treated the group to drinks there instead of at the club. I just wanted a change of scene after getting whupped so bad. And by both women to boot."

She studied his face. Nothing seemed different. His eyes softened with the same look of adoration he had shown from their college days. Surely he was telling her the truth. She smiled, rose, laid the paper on the bedside table, picked up his clothes and said, "Well, next time let me know if you're going out on the town and Buddy and I can meet you. I'd love to meet the ladies who beat you at golf all the time. And will you please learn to put your things in the hamper?"

He laughed. "Probably not." He reached out, pulled the armload of clothes from her arms, stuffed the wad under his right arm, and wrapped his left around her. "I love you," he whispered.

"Don't go getting romantic now. Buddy's bringing his new girl for supper and I have to get busy fixing it."

He released her. "I'll put them in the hamper."

"Put some pants on, Carl, before you go tromping down to the laundry room." She punched his shoulder, turned and headed for the kitchen.

I don't know if I can believe him. I'll play detective next Sunday.

She did not wait until Sunday to begin. The next day she went to the

Best Western and strode in as if she belonged. No one paid her any heed. Everywhere the cleaners were at work, their carts sitting on outside walkways or in the halls. Alone.

She spotted what she would need, lifted it, and hoped it would still be good the next week.

Tuesday evening, while Carl worked late in a conference that she knew would go on until well after dark, she ventured into the sleazy section of town and purchased the one other thing she would need if her hunch was correct.

After church the next Sunday, as Carl drove the family home, she said, "Stop at the Pizza Joint. Let's have pizza today. I don't want to cook."

Carl turned to stare at her. "Pizza? You going to eat pizza? That's different. Okay, my lady. You're in charge of the food. I'll play pickup dinner today. You got plans for while I'm at golf?"

"Kinda. I'm going to the museum. They have a new exhibit and the opening begins at 2:00 today. I know you have no interest, so I asked a friend to go. I'm driving."

As they ate pizza, Buddy asked, "Mama, did you remember to take your gluten pills?"

"Damn, no," she lied. "I better get them now." She got up from the table, went to the bedroom and returned in minutes to eat another slice.

Carl left to play golf and Buddy headed off to pick up his girlfriend to go to a movie. She walked to her car in her church outfit to go to the museum.

For four hours, she moved about the museum, chatted with various people including the artist, who introduced her to the mayor and two members of city council and three of his buyers.

She complained to the artist and one of his buyers of a stomach upset and where was the lady's room?

Instead of the lady's room, she returned home, changed into casual slacks, tennis shoes and knit top. She changed her hairdo, checked the contents of her shoulder bag to be sure she had both items, put on large circular dark glasses, picked up the Sunday *Times* and left.

At the local Best Western, she settled into a heavy stuffed chair in the lobby, her back to the registration desk, opened the paper and began to work the crossword puzzle. Her timing was nearly perfect. In less than twenty minutes, she heard his voice. She touched the hearing aid in her right ear and easily heard the conversation as the volume increased.

"That'll be seventy dollars, Mr. Sims. Room 413."

"Do you mind cash?" she heard Carl say.

"No, of course not. Let me get your receipt."

A few moments later, she heard them walk away. She waited another fifteen minutes, removed her hearing aids, gathered up her bag and newspaper, dropped the paper into the waste bin, and went to the elevators. She rode to the fourth floor, strode down the hall, and used her stolen digital key to open the door to room 413.

They were in bed. "Oh, Carl?" she said.

Their movements stopped. He turned toward her. She pointed the pistol to his head. The weight of the silencer did not hinder her aim.

She fired twice, once for him, once for her, dropped the weapon into her bag, turned and left the room. No one was in the hall. She took the elevator down, walked out, drove to the river, parked near the bridge, walked to the bank and threw the gun, silencer and digital card into the water. She watched to be sure everything fell into the current.

She backtracked: Home, Sunday outfit, museum.

Her friend said, "You okay?"

"Sorry. I hated to be gone so long. But you know how it is. My gluten pills didn't work today. Didn't stop the effects of the gluten in that pizza I had for lunch. I can't seem to stop this diarrhea. It's not the first time I've had to sit on the john for almost an hour, but I think I'm okay now. Did I miss anybody?"

"No, not anybody special."

"Carl said he would take his golf friends to supper, so let's us go get a steak and salad at Ruby Tuesday's."

Vernon said, "Sounds good. Now all that's behind us, we can get married as soon as the hullabaloo dies down."

WHAT'S IN A NAME?

She sat down at her computer to write her story and faced the same problem she always did. What names to use? Although her story was fiction, she planned to base it on the family stories of an ancestor who had fought in the early Indian wars and traveled to several of the historic forts in the early west, Fort Pitt, Fort Duquesne and often returned to his birthplace, Fort Henry.

Her ancestor, the protagonist, and his younger female cousin had been captured by Shawnees and hauled off into the woods. Hands bound, they were forced to march so rapidly the young girl dropped with exhaustion. A Shawnee lifted her, threw her over his shoulder, and they continued their hurried hike into the unknown wilderness.

The story would flow. She never had a problem with her fingers walking over the keyboard as fast as her mind worked. But she always seemed to be mentally dead and in a dither when she had to come up with a name. She stopped writing after only a few sentences. She couldn't continue to refer to the boy as *he* or *the boy,* or the girl as *she* or *the cousin.*

But what name to give them? She didn't want to use Bartholomew, her own ancestor's name, or his cousin's real name, Elizabeth-Anne, just in case she changed some events from reality and some smart student somewhere in the future decided to fact-check her story. And she couldn't use any name similar to those of the residents of these forts.

She thought of other family names, and since she had an aunt named Virginia, she settled on *Georgia* for the cousin. Be easy to keep that one straight from any other female characters she introduced. Besides, she didn't want to do what she had done with one story and not discovered until the magazine editor pointed it out: She had given the main female three names without noticing the changes.

Henry would work for her hero because she was going to locate the families' homes in Fort Henry, where Bartholomew was born. Her family had always been consistent in naming children for someone either in the family or some special event or person. She had a great uncle named *Boston* who had named his daughter *Atlanta.*

So Henry and Georgia it would be.

For a last name she doodled surnames that came to her. But Smith, Brown and Jones would not do. *How about—? That's it. Howe. No, it won't work. I can't have Henry Howe. It's too alliterative. But I do like it. I'll keep Howe anyhow.* She smiled at her thought.

She pushed back from her computer, stood, and walked around the room. Nothing came to her. She went into her back yard, into her small vegetable garden and saw the resident box turtle dining on a fallen tomato.

"That's it. Turtle. No Tuttle. Perfect."

The chance for her characters to escape came after a week of capture when the Shawnee decided the children were too far from home to try to run away. The braves' leader had untied their hands that night and demanded Georgia cook the turkey one of them brought to camp.

That night, they waited until the campfire died down and all the warriors were sleeping.

The family story was that Henry "turtled" to his cousin and they crawled away from the Indian camp. Her characters would do the same—slip out of camp at night by crawling on all fours as slowly as a turtle.

Georgia had sneaked a knife from beside one sleeping Indian, and Henry had collected a bow and several arrows. They were free, armed and ready to plunge into the wilderness and to battle wildlife and geography as they struggled to find home.

Having never lived in the Ohio lands, she could not imagine the flora and fauna of the 1700s. Chestnut trees had to have covered the land at that time. Deer, wild turkey, and of course foxes, bobcats and even bison were supposed to have lived in the area. She went online and researched what the dangers children would face as they struggled to find their way home.

It had taken Bartholomew and Elizabeth-Anne three weeks to get back to their parents. She couldn't let her hero and his cousin get home any sooner.

The story finished, she edited, tightened it, and laid it aside for a few days while she queried several magazines. One asked to see the manuscript, and a few days later she received an email:

I take it you got your story from THE GREAT WEST by Henry Howe and published by George Tuttle. You should never name characters for your historical reference sources.

She had never heard of the book, the author or the publisher.

THE WEDDING

Wynona stared out her bedroom window while thoughts of Blake, her sister and past weeks jumbled her mind. A week ago, her older sister, Tiffany, had charged into Wynona's room with the news. Blake had proposed and they were getting married.

Today. In three hours.

And three months ago he had proposed to her.

Outside, the maple leaves filtered the autumn sun and turned the world crimson. The light breeze caressed the leaves as if to say, "Stay. Stay." But the leaves tumbled from the tree and danced in the sunlight.

Wynona sighed. *The leaves are just like Blake. Dancing away when it should have been her wedding day.*

She turned and faced her mirror. Without direction from her mind, her hand rubbed her belly. Yesterday she had learned her own news. Not from her family doctor. Her parents thought she was in school. Instead she had asked her best friend to drive her to Macon. She had walked into the doctor's office with no appointment and only $15.00 to her name. He had given her the news and asked for her family information. She refused and had fled in tears.

She was pregnant. By Blake.

Her mind couldn't seem to put that day behind her. He was so handsome in his uniform. Tall, dark hair, dark eyes, dimples even when he didn't smile. He had not seen the war. Truman had authorized the bombs two days after Blake fell in boot camp and busted his leg. Six weeks later, he was discharged and returned home with a limp.

But he wore his uniform any chance he could. Nobody cared. He had volunteered and everybody in town considered him one of the war heroes even if he hadn't seen combat or even passed boot camp.

Oh how handsome he was that day four months ago when he came calling on her.

Why me? She had wondered. Every girl in school had drooled over him before he volunteered. And her classmates still gossiped about anyone he dated since he came home "from the war."

Mama said a man always looks good in uniform but you never know where he came from—rich or poor, merchant or bootlegger's family. But I knew where he came from.

Next to Daddy, his father's the richest man in town. But I knew he was a scoundrel. Caught driving drunk, but his daddy got him off all four times.

Mama was so right—he did look so handsome in his Marine dress-up outfit.

He had been a gentleman with her when he escorted her to parties and to the movies. Only on their fourth date did he try to kiss her. She hadn't even known how to kiss him back.

Well, I guess I learned soon enough.

She had snuggled with him in the car but the night he proposed, she had not resisted anything he wanted. His hands had felt so good all over her. They were to be married. How could she say no to anything he wanted to do?

Afterwards, he said, "Let's keep this a secret until I tell my folks. Let's tell them at Christmas. Our gift to them." She was so happy she agreed.

He did not call again. Day after day when the phone rang, she hurried to the living room. Not him.

Weeks later, she had heard his car—the broken muffler was unmistakable—and hurried to her bedroom window. The car stopped by their front walk, and Blake stepped out. Was he coming to see her? He strode up the front walk, and Wynona rushed to the stairs to go to the front door.

Tiffany was there first. Wynona stopped half-way down the stairs and listened.

"You ready?" he asked.

She did not hear her sister's reply, but Tiffany went out the door. Back upstairs in her room, Wynona watched them leave in his blue two-door 1940 Mercury.

The same car.

For her, Christmas was not to be a grand announcement but an admitting to her pregnancy.

But maybe not.

Tiffany had liked him from the get-go. Just as she had liked everything Wynona had. Her baby doll when she got one for her third birthday. The candy she collected on Halloween. Life was *let sister Tiffany have it or get a beating.*

She would never forget the time Tiffany had caught her in the woods behind the house and for no reason jumped her, pushed her onto the ground, sat on her belly. Tiffany had slammed her fists into her body over and over and then said, "Remember LSMFT? It's not just *Lucky Strike means fine tobacco*. For you it means *Lord save me from Tiffany*."

If Tiffany beat up on her and Wynona complained to Mama, she got the whipping because Tiffany would state firmly that Wynona had started the fight. What was Tiffany to do but defend herself?

Mama and Daddy both believed Tiffany, no matter what. They saw her as an older protective and devoted sister. In public she was truly the Tiffany of perfection like the priceless glassware she was named for. Wynona alone knew her sister as a manipulator and liar.

I reckon Blake and Tiffany really deserve each other. But like the preacher's always preaching, in hellfire.

She would give Tiffany and Blake the comeuppance they deserved.

Clad in blue jeans, tennis shoes and a light sweater, she skipped down the stairs and left the house. She was back in less than an hour, plenty of time to get ready for the wedding.

Couldn't be late. After all, she was to be the maid of honor.

Everyone who was anyone in town had come. As mayor, Daddy had invited every storeowner, every insurance agent, every banker and announced a half-day holiday for the community. The church was jammed with people. Pews designed for twenty overflowed with twenty-five.

The October day had warmed into the 80s and the electric fans standing alongside the outer aisles only stirred the heat.

Sweat beaded on everyone's forehead. Suit coats were getting damp. Ladies fanned themselves with a variety of hand-held fans—some cardboard advertising the funeral home, some dainty folding fans of pink or flowered paper or lace. Perfumes floated as the fans moved the heat.

The wedding began.

Wynona obeyed her instructions, but walked down the aisle without looking at Blake. Behind her came her father and sister.

Oh how Daddy's going to be humiliated in front of the entire town. He probably won't even get ten votes in the next election. Mama will be devastated.

And I don't care. Mama and Daddy ignored my hurt all my life. They can just face it all, along with Tiffany and Blake's parents.

She waited for the moment. Her hands trembled. Her insides knotted. But when it came, she was icy calm.

"Does anyone have reason these two should not wed? If so, speak now or forever hold your peace."

Wynona turned to face half-way between the audience and the preacher. Her voice boomed over the whumping of the standing fans and the swish of the ladies' fans. Her words echoed from the back wall.

"I object. I am carrying Blake's child. As all of you know, I am only fifteen. I don't want my baby's father to be its uncle. And I'm not about to marry him. Sheriff Bryce, are you here?"

Mother fainted.

Father charged forward and began beating Blake.

Sheriff Bryce and a deputy managed to pull the mayor off the groom. They handcuffed Blake and dragged the bloody-faced, uniformed non-Marine up the center aisle.

THE MISFIT

The all-white crowd began to stir. The race would soon begin and the noise increased. Excitement roared. They knew the winner would take all. Each one stretched, flexed, and prepared. It was win. Or die.

Outside, voices rumbled. The chamber throbbed with the excitement flooding from outside as they waited for the starting gate to snap open.

A dark figure appeared in the crowd and began to thread its way forward, toward the chamber exit. "Hey, where'd you come from?" one of the white figures asked.

The crowd turned to the dark one. "This is an all-white crowd," one said and shoved against the misfit. "How in hell did you get here?"

"Oh," the misfit replied, "I can you assure it wasn't from hell. It was from pure delight. Same way you got here."

Silence for a moment. The chamber pulsed. A faint light shimmered. An apparent leader blocked the exit and finally spoke.

"You don't belong here. You got no business in this race. Get behind the rest of us."

Outside, the noises grew more frantic. The leader spoke again. "Like I said, get back."

The misfit chuckled. "No way, Jose."

Another voice came from somewhere in the crowd. "Where *did* you come from? We've not seen you or any of your kind before. You're blacker than darkness. Why even the outside can't make you white."

The leader slipped away from the exit, moved forward and stopped before the misfit.

"You aren't going to win this race anyway and then you'll be dead. You might as well just go over to a corner and die now and save yourself all the effort of running. Why, there're enough of us to keep you from even getting through the starting gate."

"Oh, I don't see any corners here. Looks like a round room to me. Let's see, maybe I can find a corner."

The misfit began to circle as if seeking a corner. Others moved out of his way. As he neared the exit, several moved toward the exit to block him.

"Tell you what, guys. Y'all just sit yourselves down and I'll tell you the true tale of how I got here. There's no need for you to carry on like this. I have as much right as you. After all, I probably have more right.

I'm sure some of your ancestors lynched some of mine."

Noises from outside drowned out the angry groans. No one settled down.

"Sounds like things are about to get started outside, but we still got a long time before the race is going to start. Now you go on and settle down. I can't talk to you if you keep on moving around like this and shoving each other. Can't you hear? They're just beginning to get serious about us out there. Be a long time before we have to run."

General movement slowed and stopped. The misfit began to move around again as he spoke. At first, he maintained a conversation tone, but soon he became flamboyant. He gripped them with his voice, as Churchill and Kennedy had ensnared their audiences. He alone stirred. He wandered among them, and gradually made his way to the starting gate.

"My people have always been here, just like you. But we just stayed in the shadows, just like all you white guys forced us to. I come from a long line of the safety-conscious after my naughty ancestor got real naughty. He fell in love with one of your kind. He wasn't drunk. And if he were, being drunk would be no excuse. But they met one night, him and that pretty young barmaid. She strode out the door of the inn, and because she loved him too they went off into the dark, with no lantern to light their way. Only a partial moon making blue shadows on the snow. Think about it. Forbidden love back more than two hundred years ago. A cold dark night, the snow and cold keeping everyone else inside to stay warm by their fires. No street lights. No patrols. Only yourselves and love. She was not afraid. She led him down that mile-long pathway, through the deep woods, to her small cabin with nothing to guide her in the darkness but her love. Afterwards, of course, she was pregnant. Your kind cast her out and lynched him when her baby came. With nowhere else to go, she went to live with her lover's mother, and they reared the girl child together. It took way more than a hundred years and about ten generations for one of the down-line sons to pass for white. Weren't many of us left then. And I'm the only one here, so you see, I just have to win this race."

He backed to the starting gate while the crowd floated motionless.

The emotional explosion outside opened the starting gates and the misfit sped through, far ahead of the rest of the sperm, to victory and to life.

THE MILKY WAY

Millie did not know what she saw when she lay down to sleep. Nor did she know when the visions began and didn't care. Going to sleep had been preceded by these visions from before she could remember. She just let the scenes float like awake-dreams when she closed her eyes.

After her family trip to the beach when she as seven, she began to associate some of the visions with the beach, with the white sands of the beach floating as separate crystals in a never-ending mass of sparkles.

Other times, it was like seeing the Milky Way as she saw it two years later, when her parents took her on a trip west, where on the Arizona desert she felt she could reach up and not only touch the stars but also stir them around in the Milky Way.

When she stood on the edge of the Grand Canyon on her tenth birthday, she turned to her father and asked, "Where are the Anasazi dwellings?"

"The who?" her father said.

"The Anasazi," she repeated.

Her mother answered. "No, Millie, they are not here. The Anasazi dwellings are in Canyon de Chelly. Why do you ask?"

She shrugged. "I dunno. It just came in my head to ask. Are we going there?"

"Not on this trip," her mother said. " You'll get to visit the people another time."

In the third week back at school that fall, Millie was on the ninth question of an algebra test she found dreadfully simple when the classroom door opened and the principal entered. Millie looked up, laid her pencil down, shook her head, and picked it up again, but sat still and waited for the principal to speak.

She closed her eyes. The stars appeared and rolled across her vision. Her mother appeared in the stars and floated away into the distance.

"Millie? Would you come out of the class a minute?" the principal asked.

She gathered up her books, walked to the front of the class, and laid her test paper on the teacher's desk. "I'm sorry, but I haven't finished."

"You can finish—" the teacher began.

"No, Daddy won't let me come back for a week. Mama's gone."

"What do you mean?" the teacher asked.

The principal shook her head. "I'll take care of her. Come on, Millie."

She turned and followed the principal out of the room.

"I know Mama's gone away, but she's not dead," Millie said.

The principal stopped, turned and stared at Millie. "What do you mean?"

Millie shrugged. "I dunno. I just know she's not dead."

"Well, your father called and said he was coming to pick you up. He didn't mention your mother. I surely hope everything is all right."

On the drive home, Father told her Mother had not shown up at her job this morning, her car was found near the cemetery but empty. They were hoping the kidnappers would call. He wanted her home with him to be sure they did not kidnap her too.

"She hasn't been kidnapped," Millie said. "She's gone to the stars."

"No, Millie, don't talk that way. She's not dead. We'll find her."

Millie closed her eyes against her father's words. Again she saw her mother rising like an eagle on the updrafts, the Milky Way wrapping around her like a glittering shawl.

Two weeks passed with no call from kidnappers, and the police had been unable to find any trace of her.

On the fifteenth day, Millie told her father, "You know as well as I do Mama's not going to come home. I need to go back to school."

Ten years later, at nineteen and already a senior at the university, with a 4.0 average in astrophysics, she was eating lunch in the cafeteria with her classmate Brady, who competed with her for the highest grade ratio in the class. She looked across the room at a professor sitting alone.

"Who is that?" she asked and pointed. "The one by himself."

The images floated into view, shadowing the man. She saw him as an old hunched-backed man who could not sit erect.

"Which one? The redhead with the pony tail?"

"Yes."

"That's Professor Thompson. He's in charge of the Rhesus studies. He doesn't get here often. He's mostly at the wildlife site."

"Ashamed for him to have his last meal alone," she muttered.

"What? What did you say?"

"Look at him. He's dying. He'll be dead before classes end today."

"Naw, you're just rambling about nothing. Why, he's not even fifty. He runs in all the local races. He ran the ten K last week. He's healthy as a horse. Just look at him."

She shrugged. "Well, I got to get to my one o'clock class." She gathered up her trash, rose, dumped it in the trash bin, and went to class.

A half-hour later, an ambulance roared up to the science building, Siren screaming and lights flashing. Everyone in class, including the professor, went to the window that overlooked the front entrance circular driveway.

Minutes later, the EMTs emerged with Professor Thomson on a gurney.

Three hours later, the bulletin boards throughout the university bore the notice of the professor's death.

Graduation came. Her 4.0 average tied her with Brady's 4.0 for the valedictorian speech. She declined. Her excuse that she would not be able to inspire the class in any direction but astrophysics. Let Brady have the honor since he was an eloquent speaker and had led the debate team to victory statewide.

Two nights later, the visions came again. Millie lay with eyes closed and watched the sand storms turn into stars. She felt a voice praising her and asking if she would join them. The urge to go to *wherever* pulled her. She agreed in her mind. To visit these illusions would solve the mystery of *why me* that had haunted her since childhood.

She awoke in another bed. In another structure with a clear dome for a roof. She stood, walked to the edge of the dome. The Milky Way did not flow only overhead—it surrounded the structure as she remembered it wrapping around her mother.

Behind her came her mother's voice. "Welcome home, Little Eagle. Welcome to *Anasazi Starship Four*."

THE ASSASSIN

He was bench pressing and the two-hundred-pound weights were extended overhead when the cell phone rang in the pocket of his sweat pants. He had learned a long time back to never let it be out of reach. The barbells clanked down.

"Hello? Ryan here."

"Ryan, I have another problem and I need you."

"Yes, Sir?"

"Come to the office. Not over the phone."

"On my way, Sir."

He was five miles from the office and sweaty. He needed a shower and fresh clothes. You don't go to the White House stinking of sweat and not in a suit.

He was immediately admitted into the office where he stood at attention as if a soldier reporting to a senior officer.

The president rose, came to stand before him and smiled. "At ease, soldier."

He smiled back and relaxed.

"Whatcha need me to do, Sir?"

"I have a problem with a reporter. Jeff Kenson. He's getting too close. If he is able to dig much deeper we'll be in trouble. I think he's been in touch with Janice."

Janice. Oh gawd, if the word leaks out he's shacking up with her again, he'll be in real trouble. Like he was when he was my lieutenant."

"You want me to..." He pointed his forefinger to his temple.

The president nodded and named the reporter and the amount he would pay. "It needs to be handled today, before he has time to get the article into the *Post*."

"You got it, Sir." The sergeant-cum-problem-solver left the office and the White House and considered his options.

I could be an informer. Anonymous, of course. Or maybe not. Tell him I know about Janice and can verify information. Maybe tell him I have some pictures. Let him know I served with POTUS. I'm broke and need money. Tell him I'll need $10,000 for the pictures. Make a bit extra.

Meet him at the bridge. Give him a shove, and let Gabe take care of the remains and no one will ever find him.

He headed home to prepare for the assignment. On the way, seven miles down the dirt road leading to his farm home, he stopped on the bridge over the river, climbed out of the car, and leaned over the railing.

Yep, ole Gabe is there. He needs something to eat. Been a while since I threw him something special.

The eleven-foot gator basked in the sun on the bank, his mouth slightly open. Ryan slapped the railing and clucked as if getting a horse to gallop. "See ya, Gabe ole fella. Bring you a good meal soon."

Ratty clothing could be a help. Convince the reporter I'm broke and need money. Take a briefcase for the pictures that don't exist. Nobody knows POTUS and I are still in touch. I could go to the apartment and suicide him. But no. No pistol this time. The last suicide with a bullet in the back of the head was hard to get by the medical examiner. Besides, his condo has security cameras. Be hard to get in and out and not be noticed.

He gathered what he might need. Two throwaway cell phones. An unregistered off-the-street pistol, just in case. Nothing else.

He looked like a street bum when he walked from his house. His clothes sagged as if he had lost thirty pounds since they fit. Makeup smeared across his face made it look as he had not bathed in weeks. He had pasted a fake thin beard over his chin. *Mama would not even know me now.*

Kenson was well known as a fact digger.

He stood in the yard and called the reporter's home. When Kenson answered his land line, Ryan said, "I got you some tips on a lady friend of the POTUS. And pictures. Meet me on Shady Trails, at the bridge. In one hour. That'll be three p. m. Don't try to be smart and get there early and set up a hidden camera. I'll wait till ten minutes after. We'll be so far off the grid nobody'll be around. I can't be seen with you or I'll be killed."

"What? Who are you?"

"Somebody you know. We were in college together. You wouldn't remember me. I was a nobody while you were school paper editor. Meet me. I got the connection you need for what you're working on. And like I said earlier, I got pictures."

"How do you know what I'm working on?"

Ryan chuckled. "I know."

"What is the project? Let me know you really know something."

He almost said *suicide by bullets in the back of the head.* "Janice. I'll wait at the bridge for you. Three sharp. I won't wait longer than ten minutes. I may be followed so you won't even see my car. If you're not there on time, I'll be gone and you won't hear from me again."

He closed the phone and slipped it into a pocket. He would throw it into the river after he dumped the reporter in.

He hiked to the river and stood in the shadow of a white oak seventy yards from the bridge. He had stood there before when he had other such meetings with other threats to his lieutenant. A slight breeze rustled the leaves. A fox slipped from the brush at the far end of the bridge, stopped in the middle of the road, looked both ways and trotted into the woods.

Ryan smiled. It was probably the mama fox with the den in his back yard where she was raising a litter of four kits. He needed to throw Gabe another chicken when he got home.

Twenty minutes later, Kenson drove up to the bridge, stopped on the far end where the fox had crossed, turned off his car and stepped out. He stood beside the car for a minute, glanced at his watch.

Ha. I figured he'd be early. Let him wait and wonder.

After about a minute, the reporter strolled onto the bridge and looked down at the stream. Ryan sized him up. Kinda bulky, but most of it was probably that fancy suit he had on. And glasses he pushed up three times as Ryan watched. Kenson stopped and leaned on the railing. Ryan knew he was looking at the alligator.

At two minutes to three, Ryan approached with the briefcase in his left hand. Kenson glanced at him and then continued to look into the river.

"You got an extra dollar?" Ryan asked and grinned.

The reporter looked up at him. "No, but if you're hungry, I can take you to McDonald's and buy you something to eat. But not right now. Why don't you walk on down to the highway and I'll pick you up in a bit?"

Ryan shrugged. "I hope you got the ten thousand."

"You're the one who called?"

"Yeah. I need some money. Whatcha seeing down there?" He moved over beside the reporter, switched the briefcase to his other hand and set it down by his right foot, away from the reporter.

The reporter turned back toward the river and pointed. "Down there. Over by that backwater pool. There's an alligator. Somebody must have brought it up from Florida and when it got too big for a house pet they turned it loose in the river."

"That's Old Gabe. Everybody throws him something to eat. I'm glad you got here on time." Ryan extended his right hand. No one refused an offered handshake.

One more suicide, and this one not even with two bullets in the head. Just a quick dive into the alligator pool. End of that story of the prez and the prostitute.

The reporter looked at the extended hand and frowned slightly. But he gripped Ryan's hand. For a second, it became a macho squeezing contest. Ryan saw Kenson's eyes change and knew the reporter realized he was about to die. Ryan smiled.

Ryan jerked Kenson toward him. To his astonishment, the reporter lunged forward with the pull. Ryan tried to recover his balance but Kenson slammed his shoulder into Ryan's hip, grabbed Ryan's thighs, and lifted Ryan's upper body over the rail.

Ryan flailed and tried to grab the railing as he fell face forward. Gabe watched, and before Ryan hit the water Gabe lunged in for the free meal.

Kenson shook his head. *Too bad I can't write this story about the president's paid assassin. It's a sure Pulitzer winner, far better than some slutty story about the president's mistress.*

THE EMTs AND MRS. MURPHY

For the third time in less than a week, the alarm rang in the fire station and the emergency medical technicians dashed to the ambulance. The familiar address told them Mrs. Murphy needed help again. This time, the fire truck stayed in the station and only Wilma and Jerry, two EMTs, took the call.

The old lady would be on the floor. Seemed like she got up to go to the john in the middle of the night and for some reason couldn't keep her feet under her knees.

Still, they went with lights flashing. Wilma told Jerry to forget the stretcher. All they needed to do was get her on her feet again. At the front door, Wilma remembered the code to open the lock hanging on the door knob; she set the combination and removed the front door key. She opened the door to a house in darkness. No light anywhere, just like before. She found the light switch by the door and flicked it on. The living room looked unchanged from her two previous visits.

As she exited the living room into the hall, she again flicked on a light. She and Jerry hurried down the hall toward the bedroom. Blackness seemed to seep from the bedroom door.

She felt for the light switch, found it, clicked it on and saw the old lady sprawled on the floor on her back. And not exactly decent, but more so than on the last visit when she wore only a short tee shirt and white cotton undies. Tonight, at least the tee shirt was down to her knees and Wilma could only assume she wore undies—nothing showed otherwise.

"Fallen again, Mrs. Murphy?"

"You know, something is going on here. I was walking back to the bedroom and the next thing I know, I'm waking up on the floor. How come I keep on falling? It's only when I get up in the middle of the night. I don't have the problem when I get up in the morning. In fact, during the day I tend to the farm. I cut my own firewood. I milk the cow and churn my own butter. I even mended fences today. If I've got to fall, why not out there, toting a chain saw or swinging a maul to split logs or kindling?"

"Maybe you are still half asleep when you get up in the night."

"Oh, no. I'm wide awake. After the first time I ease up real slow, turn on the bedside lamp and even the overhead."

The EMTs looked at each other. "You turned on the light? None were on. Not even one light in the house."

"Maybe I turned the overhead light off on the way back to bed. I can't think I would have turned the bedside light off until I got into the bed. But I just can't remember anything but walking from the bathroom and waking up here on the floor. And not being able to get up. My lord, Wilma, I get up from the ground with an armload of wood with no trouble. Here I can barely move. It's like I am hexed or something." She smiled at her own words, paused, and continued.

"Actually, I think I am hexed, like I told you before."

Wilma smiled back. "Well, let's get you on your feet and back to bed." Wilma held a hand down and Mrs. Murphy took it. Jerry stepped behind Mrs. Murphy and as Wilma pulled her up into a sitting position he slid his hands under her armpits and lifted.

Mrs. Murphy stood and smiled. "Well if I was conjured, at least I was able to call you. Or did I call you? No, I couldn't have. My phone is on the other side of the bed." She frowned. "How did you know I needed you?"

"You called 911."

"From the floor? No." She turned to look across the bed. "See? There's my phone."

"I thought—don't you have one of the safety alert buttons?" Wilma asked.

"No. I might not remember what happened, but who turned off the lights? I always leave the hall light on at night just in case the bedside light bulb goes out."

"The house was dark as pitch when we got here. Same as the last two times. You sure you are not sleep walking?"

"Oh, posh! No. If that was it, I'd be able to get up. I'm strong as a stubborn mule. But when this happens, I can't do anything. I'm as limp as an old wet plow line."

"Well, you let us just tuck you in and we'll lick up the front door as we leave."

Mrs. Murphy crawled into bed and grinned. "Y'all putting me to bed just like my Pa used to do. Jerry, aren't you going to tuck me in and kiss me on the forehead too, like Pa used to do? You remind me of Pa the way you take care of me."

"Sure, Mrs. Murphy." He leaned over to buss her on the forehead and as he did so, his body slipped to the floor as if his bones had melted.

"Jerry!" Wilma shouted. "What's the matter?" She knelt beside him.

Mrs. Murphy sat up. "He's been hexed too. I told you and that other partner you brought the first time, there's a conjurer here."

Jerry opened his eyes and looked up to see Wilma staring down at him and felt the pressure of the cuff on his arm. "What happened?"

"You just turned into a wet noodle and went down. Blood pressure's only 90 over 50. No wonder you collapsed. You've got to see a doctor."

Watching, Mrs. Murphy leaned over the side of the bed. "Give him a few minutes. The conjurer got to him is all."

Wilma looked up at her. "Mrs. Murphy, how come you keep on talking about a conjurer?"

"I see her." She pointed to the mirror over her dresser. "Look a-there. See her?"

Wilma looked to where she pointed.

A black-clad figure with a hood covering its face shimmered like a Halloween figure trembling in the October breeze and seemed to watch over the room.

"I told y'all so. Ain't a thing wrong with me. Just do what I asked you the first time. Take that darn old mirror outta here and bust it up."

The figure faded into the reflection of the room.

THE CONCERT

Cassie was late and would barely have time to get her tickets and find Pauline before the concert started. The line stretched from the door, down the steps and two blocks along the street. It would take her a half-hour to work her way up to the "will call" window and pay for her and Pauline's tickets.

Word had circulated rapidly among the gay and lesbian community that last night's performance was special. It had been a salute to Harvey Milk on the anniversary of his murder. At least half of the local LGTB population and probably half from across the southeast were here tonight. She recognized many of her fellow members in line, but she would have to give up her space or break ahead to chat with those she knew.

She jounced in place as the line inched forward. She noticed a man walking toward the front door without regard to the line. He carried a case. Wore a beard. Looked like an Arab.

My god, he's a terrorist. We got to stop him from going inside. That has to be one of those bombs or even a broken-down shotgun. She turned to the nearest man in line behind her and spoke her thoughts.

"I don't want to get involved," he said.

"If you don't get involved out here you'll go inside and be a victim. Help me stop him."

He shook his head. "I dunno."

"Give me your tie, then," she demanded and reached toward his chest.

He laughed "What do you think you're going to do? Tie him up?"

"No, I'll just grab him from behind. Let me have it."

He jerked it off. She grabbed it and ran toward the stranger.

She approached behind him as he reached the steps. With one motion, she flipped the tie over his head and jerked it tight against his throat.

"Somebody help me," she yelled as he shoved his free hand up and grabbed at the tie. "He's a terrorist. He's got a bomb or a shotgun."

No one moved. The man kept pulling at the tie. He jerked it so hard she stumbled. He freed his neck and stammered, "Let me go. This is my trumpet, you idiot. And here," he shoved something into her face.

A badge, with his photograph, name and the emblem of the orchestra.

"Oh, man, I'm so sorry. You just looked like..."

"I know what I look like. I am a Muslim. I was born here. I am a professional musician. Now get out of my way. I am supposed to accompany the chorus tonight."

He glared at her. His eyes seemed black, intense, angry. His jaw muscles pulsed. She backed away.

"I'm so sorry. I just thought—they tell us if we see something, we should do something."

"Doing something doesn't mean to attack people. If I were a terrorist, I would have already killed you. You need killing anyway, a woman dressed like you, showing your face to everyone. And one of these queers to boot."

He turned and walked away.

She started back toward the line and realized everyone stared at her. *No way I'm going in there now. I'm getting out of here.*

She almost ran to her car. Once inside her red Mazda, she propped her hands on the steering wheel and realized she still gripped the tie. She flung it out the window, wrapped her arms around the steering wheel, and rested her head on her forearms. *Oh, Pauline, I'm so sorry. I hope no one connected you with me. I hope you can pick up the tickets. Oh, dear Gussie, they are in my name. Maybe you can get them and enjoy the concert. It's the only time I've gotten us front row seats.*

She straightened up, took a deep breath, and called Pauline on her cell phone. No answer. She left a message, "I've run into a problem and can't make the show. They should let you have the tickets. Please call me when the show is over. Love you."

She cranked the car. Home at last, she pulled a Coors Light from her fridge and sat down to find a TV program she hadn't seen before. Nat Geo showed lions killing. Animal Planet was a tree house. She clicked off the TV, went to her disk player, shook her head before she even turned it on.

I got to get out of here. I feel like I'm trapped in the apartment. I got to get out, get out, get out. I've never had claustrophobia before. I'll go down to the Otherside.

Cassie had not been to the lesbian bar since she and Pauline had been dating. At least there she would be among friends, some of whom she hadn't met, she thought. It beat sitting alone at home and feeling sorry about humiliating herself in front of so many people.

The bar's lot was full. Everybody who wasn't at the concert was here tonight. She slid out of the car, left it with the valet and entered the bar. Smoke stung her eyes. The overhead lights spun colors across the room. The dance floor trembled with the pounding of music and feet.

She wove through the crowd to the bar and recognized Dusty, still on duty—about ten years now. She leaned on an open corner and waited for Dusty to notice her.

"Hadn't seen you in a long time," Dusty said. "You still with Pauline or you on the prowl?"

She half-smiled. "I guess a little of both. She's at the concert. We had a mix-up. Anyhow, I just couldn't stay home tonight so I thought I'd come down here, have a beer, stay sober enough to drive home and call Pauline after the concert."

"What's your poison?"

She ordered a draft, placed her cash on the bar, turned, leaned back, and watched the dancers. Dusty said, "Here you go," placed the mug on the bar, and picked up the cash.

Cassie sipped her beer, in no hurry to leave and with no interest in a conversation with someone who would think she was looking for a night together. When she finished her beer, she checked the time. At least another hour before the concert would end. She decided to have another beer. She chatted with Dusty when the bartender was free. By eleven, she decided it was time to head home.

As she said goodnight to Dusty, her phone vibrated and she pulled it from her pocket. She said, "It's Pauline. See ya later."

She pressed the icon to answer but could hear almost nothing. "Hold on a second," she said and pushed her way through the crowd and out the door. Outside was quiet except for some late-night traffic and somewhere far off the blare of sirens.

"Okay, I'm where I can hear you now. Are you still at the concert? It's so noisy. Did you have fun? See anybody we know?"

"Who is speaking please?"

"Who are you? What are you doing with Pauline's phone?"

"I'm trying to reach the In Case of Emergency person for this phone."

"Oh my God. It *was* a bomb."

SISTERS IN THE NIGHT

Charlotte put on her sluttish outfit for the fifth night, checked the contents of the imitation leather bag for the third time and left for the evening. She drove across town and parked around the corner a block away from the sisters' corner.

She joined the sisters of the night for the fifth evening and chatted with Tiny tonight. The prostitute was beautiful, with a soft complexion that radiated youth and had not yet been hardened by her profession.

A car pulled up, the passenger window rolled down. The man inside did not speak for a moment as he surveyed the seven women. They watched him.

Charlotte saw hope on each of the seven faces as they waited for the potential customer to decide.

A hand extended, a finger pointing to Tiny.

She turned to Charlotte, said "Business. I gotta go."

Tiny stepped to the car, leaned slightly and spoke too softly for Charlotte to hear the conversation. After a moment, she opened the door, slid into the passenger seat and closed the door.

Seems like every time I start a good interview for my series, the lady goes off on business.

She watched the silver BMW pull away.

It was not one of the cars she had seen before in her research study. As she had each time one of the girls left the corner with a John, she pulled out her note pad, wrote the time, the girl, the car make, model, color and tag number.

"Howcome you always write down something when one of us goes out on business?" Jewel asked.

Charlotte slid her note pad back into the purse hanging over her shoulder. "I just worry about all of you. All of us girls if... Well, you know."

One by one, the other four girls left with Johns and Charlotte was alone. Midnight, and she was alone on the most dangerous corner in town. She pulled her Smith&Wesson model 617 .22 caliber revolver from the holster strapped to her thigh at top of her hose beneath her short skirt. She gripped it with her hand hanging down by her side as she strode to her car. No solicitations. Ten minutes later, she was on her way home.

The next night, she was back on the corner as twilight fell. Same group. All except Tiny.

She continued her chatting with the girls, swapping her lies for their half-truths or perhaps truths.

After an hour, she asked Jewel, who seemed to know all of the girls, their histories and where they stayed, "Howcome Tiny's not here tonight?"

"I dunno. It ain't like her. She needs the money. You know she's working this just to pay her way in college. Said them student loans folks own you forever. This way she pays as she goes."

A bright yellow Caddy parked and a tall, thin black man exited from the driver's side. Charlotte could only think of his stride as a strut. He carried an unlit cigar in his left hand. Three gold chains hug around his neck, outside his pink shirt collar. She couldn't help but notice the rings glittering on the hand holding the cigar.

He stopped in front of her and poked the cigar at her. "You been here five nights I know of and I ain't seen you before then. Who you working for? This here is mine and Jenkins corner."

"Ha. None of your business. Who you working for?"

"I works for me. So do two of these here ladies. And two of 'em work for Jenkins. He say you don't work for him. So you gonna be working for me. You understand?"

"I don't work for you, whoever you are. You didn't even tell me your name."

"Don'tcha go giving me no sass. You give me what you take in and I see you got a place to stay and three meals a day."

"I got myself a place to stay, and I manage to eat three times a day, and a fourth time if I'm hungry. Get along, buster."

He slapped her. Knocked her head sideways.

She backed up, leaned against the brick wall of the abandoned building, reached under the hem of her above-the-knee outfit, and pulled out her pistol.

He looked at it. Looked back up into her eyes. "You gonna pay for that, Missy. That there peashooter ain't gonna hurt me none."

"Oh?"

Her right leg came up, the toe of her shoe slamming into his crotch. He screamed, bent double.

"Oh God, he gonna kill you in a minute," Jewel said.

A black Crown Vic pulled up behind the Cadillac. The pimp struggled upright, glanced at the car, stumbled around to the driver's door of his, and climbed in. Tires squealed as he fled.

A woman slid from the front passenger seat of the Crown Vic.

"Uh-oh. Cops," Jewel said and turned to walk away.

The officer came around the car, looked at Charlotte, shook her head and said, "Ladies, looks like I scared off one of your pimps. Well, I'm not here about your business or his. I need some help. Some information and hope you can help. I'm not here to hassle you."

The girls hesitated. Charlotte called, "It's okay, girls. I know this cop. She says she won't hassle you, then she won't. Let's see what she's needing."

Jewel returned. "If you say so, Charlotte. After what you just done, we can take your word."

"I'm Detective Lisa Dickens," she stated. She held a folder in one hand and continued. "I'm trying to find out something about this girl. The picture isn't pretty. We found her body—well, we think she worked the streets. Do any of you know her?"

Charlotte reached over and took the picture.

"Oh dear Gussie, it's Tiny. What happened?"

The others gasped. "Oh, Tiny, Tiny," Jewel whispered and shook her head. "You ain't never gonna get your degree." She tried to wipe away her tears.

Lisa looked at Charlotte, nodded slightly and said, "It's an on-going investigation. We just need to identify her at this stage." She turned to Jewel. "You know her?"

"Yessum. But we knowed her just as Tiny. She was working to pay her schooling. She was at the college here in town."

"Do you know if she lived in the dorms or an apartment or where? Any information will help. With about five thousand students at the college, anything will help."

"I think she stayed in the dorms," Charlotte offered. "She said something one night about she had to go wherever the Johns wanted to. She couldn't take them to her place."

Jewel looked over at Charlotte, took the four steps to her, and poked her arm. "Ain't you got that there tag number I seen you write down last night? You so near crying you done forgot? You ain't never gonna make it here on the streets, honey."

"God, yes." She rummaged into her purse, removed her note pad, flipped a few pages, and found the note. "Here it is, Detective." She read the number. The detective wrote it down and then reached over for the notebook.

"Sorry, Charlotte, I know you were working on this, but your notepad is evidence in a murder investigation. I have to take it."

Charlotte pulled her notepad back, held it over her shoulder. "No. You can't take this."

Lisa said, "Come on. You realize what your note means. I have to have it." She wiggled her fingers in a "give it to me" gesture.

Charlotte sighed, shook her head, and handed over the notepad.

"You'll get it back as soon as I can release it."

Yeah, Charlotte thought. *But at least I have the voice recordings. If I tell Lisa about the voice recordings, then there goes my entire series. I won't get anything back until the trial is over and the story is too stale to write. A week in these hell-high heels and costume and there goes my week-long series on the dangers facing our destitute women who have to work the night shifts. Damn.*

"I need you to come with me, Charlotte," the detective said.

Jewel stepped between the officer and Charlotte. "She ain't got to go nowhere with you, Detective. She ain't done nothing."

"That's not it. We just need to get her official statement. She's not under arrest."

"It's okay, Jewel. I don't mind. I know the detective."

"You sure?"

Charlotte nodded. "Yes, I'm sure." She turned to the officer. "You going to make me ride in the prisoner's locked back seat?"

"Fraid so. The front seat doesn't hold but two, and my partner's sitting there." She turned to the group. "You ladies be careful. Some of these Johns can be dangerous. But then, I expect you know that."

She nodded to Charlotte and they left for the station house. Or so Charlotte thought.

Two blocks away, Lisa said, "You want to go home?"

"Home would be good. I have to write the story and I can file it from the house."

The car stopped, Lisa opened the door for Charlotte, and blocked her exit. "Okay, Charlotte. I need your recorder."

"What?"

"You heard me. Your recorder. I know you. You've probably recorded every word I've said tonight. Probably got it running right now. You know damn well it's evidence. And you sit on this story. Not a word to anyone, not even your editor, until I say so."

"Okay, okay. Just let me out of this car. The back seat smells like drunk-man's piss. But if you give out any of my information to anybody in the press, I'll never but never speak to you again, you understand me, my dear sister?"

THE MORNING AFTER

"But Daddy, I love him."

"You got no business with him. He's a buffoon. You'll be miserable."

"No, I won't. He's nice to me."

"Marry him and you'll find out how not nice he really is."

A car honked outside. "See," Daddy said, "he won't even come to the door for you."

Becky huffed, turned and scooted out the front door.

Dick grinned as she opened the door and slid in. "You hungry? I figured we might get a bite to eat."

"Sure. We haven't had supper."

His blue Chevy truck was so old it had a bench seat, and she scooted over to sit close. He draped his arm around her and she slid her hand along the tattooed pattern of black, red and orange swirls. His right ear lobe stretched under the weight of three rings.

"You got your hair cut," she said about his Mohawk.

"Yeah. Gonna get me a new tattoo on both sides and keep the hair like this. You like it?"

"Sure. It gives you distinction. It keeps you from looking like every Tom, Dick and Harry in town."

"Well, I have to look like Dick, seeing as how I am a Dick."

They laughed. He parked at Zaxby's and they walked in holding hands.

He placed their order and brought it to the table where she waited. He set the order down and reached into his pocket. He pulled out a small box, opened it, and dropped to one knee. "I er... Will you marry me?" he stammered.

The room fell silent.

She looked into the box. It held a ring that glimmered in the harsh overhead light. *A real diamond* she thought. She looked up from the ring to his eyes and saw a rich, loving future. "Oh, yes, Dick. Oh, yes, I will."

Applause broke out in the diner. He slid the ring onto her finger and she held her hand up to admire it. "It's beautiful."

"I got it from over at K's," he said and kissed her.

She heard *Kay* and thought of the commercial "Every kiss begins with Kay."

"Let's eat," he said. He scrambled up and onto his seat.

After supper, he drove to Lover's Lane and tried to coax her into sex, but she insisted they wait until they married. "Daddy'd kill me if I got pregnant."

"I'll use a condom. You won't get pregnant."

"I can't. Not till we are married."

He gave up and drove her home.

Daddy waited for her in the living room. "You're late. You were supposed to be in before ten. It's almost eleven."

"Oh, Daddy, please don't fuss. Look. He proposed. He's not trash. He gave me real diamonds, from Kay Jewelry."

"Becky, you got no business accepting a proposal. You're only seventeen."

"Well, I'm going to marry him," she huffed and stormed upstairs to her room.

When Dick arrived Saturday afternoon and honked, she hurried out. "You tell your folks?" he asked.

"Yeah. Daddy said no."

"Tell you what. You pack up a suitcase when you get home. I'll come by about midnight and we'll elope."

"Where can we find a preacher at midnight?"

"I know one. I'll arrange it and everything."

She agreed. At midnight, from her window she watched his truck ease along the street out front, and with suitcase in hand, she eased through the house and out the front door.

As she opened the truck door, he said, "Throw your suitcase in the back." She lifted it over the side and dropped it into the truck bed before she climbed into the front seat with him.

"I got the preacher lined up. We're to go to his house. Got the papers too." He patted his shirt pocket where a folded paper stuck out and extended almost to his shoulder.

He drove to a cottage at the edge of town. The porch light welcomed them, and he knocked. A thin man with a long white beard opened the door. "You Dick and Becky?" he asked.

"Sure are. Here to get wedded up," Dick replied.

The ceremony was brief, the papers signed by all, and Dick's kiss was one of possession more than love.

"Got us a real honeymoon cabin picked out," he said. He drove while she cuddled against him in the circle of his right arm. Almost an hour later, his headlights illuminated the front of a rough cabin and he stopped. "Here's our honeymoon cabin, Lovey," He pulled a large flashlight from behind the seat, got out and said "Come on. Don't just sit there. Grab your suitcase."

She slid out behind him and leaned over the back of the truck for her suitcase. "I can't reach it," she said.

"Oh, for Pete's sake, can't you do anything?" He leaned over, grabbed the suitcase, and clunked it onto the ground. "Come on," he said and strode to the front door.

She grabbed the suitcase and hurried to catch up to him and the light. Darkness seemed to reach out to grab her. She shivered, almost afraid of the loneliness and deep night.

Inside, he lit a Coleman lantern. "Don't we have electric lights?" she asked. "Where's the bathroom?"

"We got an outhouse."

"Oh, Dick, I'm scared to go outside to an outhouse in the dark."

"Well, get over it. Take the flashlight. Go down the path to your left and it'll be on your right. You can have it. I can lift my leg against a tree."

She took the flashlight, scurried outside and found the outhouse, but no toilet paper. Only a stack of hunting magazines. She laughed in spite of herself—no Sears Roebuck catalogue, but hunting magazines for toilet paper.

As soon as she was back inside, he took her hand and led her to the bedroom.

There was nothing in the room but two beds. No headboards, just mattresses on frames. The room smelled musty. The beds looked slept in, the covers tossed.

She cringed. Her suitcase stood against the wall. "Let me get my gown," she said.

"You don't need a gown. Just get naked."

"Dick!"

"Don't *Dick* me. Just get naked. And get in the bed."

He proceeded to strip. She turned her back to undress and chose the cleaner looking of the two beds. She pulled the sheet up over her. He stood by the bed and looked down.

She had never seen any male organ and as his enlarged, she became frightened.

"You don't have to be scared. It won't hurt you. You'll get used to it and love it."

But she didn't love it. His love making was not love giving but brutal taking. When it ended, she turned onto her side and cried. The pillow stank of stale sweat, old perfume and hair spray. She didn't want to think of what the smells were in the bed. The cabin was not a honeymoon cabin but a hell cabin. She wanted to go home. Daddy was right. He didn't love her.

Morning came and with it another session of brutality. When he finished, he said, "Fix me some coffee."

She didn't move. Her body ached.

"I said, fix me some coffee."

"How? There's no electricity."

"There's a wood burning stove. Get the wood from outside, build a fire, put coffee and water into a pot, and that's how you make coffee." He shoved her off the bed.

She struggled to her feet, rummaged in her suitcase for something to put on. She could not remember what she had packed. She found a pair of slacks, a pair of tennis shoes and the tee shirt she had used in another life as a pajama top.

Outside, she went first to the outhouse where she sat and cried. "Oh, Daddy, why didn't I listen to you?' she muttered to herself.

She found the woodpile and carried two pieces inside. She had no idea about how to build a fire. She told him she needed help.

He grunted, swore, "Damn stupid bitch," got up and started the fire.

In daylight, she had a better view of the cabin. A third room was nothing but bunks. It smelled as raunchy as the middle room. She hunted in the front room until she found the coffee. But no sign of water.

"There's a well outside. Draw up a bucket," he replied to her question.

"I didn't know I was supposed to be your slave."

"Yeah? Well get used to it. You're not my slave. You're just one more whore and you'll be on the street when we get back to town. I can get a hundred bucks a john for you."

She stared at him. "What are you talking about? We're married."

He laughed. "You think so?" He went to his shirt and pulled out the paper. "This is not a marriage license. It's fake. Just like that there ring. It's nothing but glass. And just like that preacher last night. You're the fifth slut he's married me to in the last two months. And you'll be my fifth girl on the street in Atlanta. Now get out to the well and draw up some water and make my coffee."

She went outside, looked around for what might be a well, and caught sight of Dick's truck. And the shotgun hanging in the rack in front of the window. She opened the truck and lifted out the shotgun. Just like one her daddy had, that he showed her the morning he wanted her to go squirrel hunting, the morning he called her squeamish because she refused to go. All you had to do was slide that wooden part backward and snap it forward, and it would be ready to shoot.

Somewhere near the trigger was the thing you push to show a red dot which would mean it was not safe to point anywhere.

She pumped the shotgun. A shell popped out, but she saw another slide into the chamber. She found the safety and slid it off. She started back to the house, changed her mind, and reached inside the truck. Three blasts on the horn brought him outside.

"What's the matter with you?" he snapped.

"You are the matter," she said. She raised the shotgun to her shoulder and looked down the top edge of the barrel. His chest showed beyond the little dot at the end of the barrel. She pulled the trigger.

The kickback almost sat her down. She staggered backwards as he fell off the porch and sprawled across the ground. She walked over, kicked him in the side, and shook her foot from the pain to her toes. But he did not move. She found the safety and pushed it back on.

"Thank you, Daddy. You wouldn't ever call me squeamish again if I could tell you. This beats shooting those squirrels. Now let me see if I can figure what I've got to do."

She went inside, stripped the bed and dumped the bedding into the back of the truck. She found all her clothing, stuffed it back into the suitcase, and carried it out and threw it into the truck with the bedding. No key in the ignition.

She grimaced at the thought of touching him, and as she reached toward his pocket, she paused. "Nope. DNA." She went back inside, found a grungy towel, and used it as a makeshift glove as she poked her hand into his pants pocket and found the keys. She left him lying where he fell and shoved the towel into the pile of bedding.

Fifteen minutes after she shot him, she was driving down the dirt road and wondered where she was. She couldn't believe how happy she had been last night, so thrilled to be married to him she had snuggled against him and never once looked to see where they were going. The long driveway ended at a paved road. She looked both ways, saw nothing to tell her which way to go, and turned right. "Right has to be right," she told herself.

Three miles down the road, she came to a bridge. She stopped midway across, slipped out and listened. No sound of a vehicle. She heard a splash and looked over the railing to see a widening circle. *Probably a fish.* She took the bedding from the back, threw it over the railing and watched it begin to float away as it soaked up water. She was sure it would soon sink, but it didn't matter. None of her DNA would be left to find after the water soaked into it.

She looked at her suitcase and pondered. *It all needs to go.* She dumped her clothing. It too soaked quickly. The bedding had floated only yards downstream and was beginning to sink. She threw the suitcase after the clothes.

Now I got to get rid of this truck. If I can figure out how. Maybe run it off the bridge. But the water's not deep enough to hide it. I could burn it, but I don't have any matches. I guess I'll have to keep on going and figure it out. At least there's nobody on the road. I hadn't even seen a house.

The road stretched between rows of planted pines for mile after mile. She considered just leaving it anywhere, but realized she needed the truck to get close enough to home to walk the last distance. She approached a crossroads. Relief flooded her. The sign pointing to her left read, "Tickleboro, 3." Home was no more than the three miles and the river was down to her right. She turned right.

So far, nobody on the road. No one at the river bridge. She stopped and considered how to get the truck under water and not have to drive it into the river herself. She tried to prop the end of the shotgun against the accelerator and the butt against the seat but it was too long to push against the front edge of the seat and wasn't long enough to prop against the back. She dropped it onto the floorboard and looked into the truck bed.

One of those long narrow boards. The two-by-four was the perfect length. She propped it against the accelerator and wedged the other end against the back of the seat.

With the door ajar, she cranked it, kept her foot on the clutch, put the gear into *drive* and turned the wheel as far as she could to the right. She jerked her foot from the accelerator and rolled through the door onto her shoulder and across the road as easily as she did in her cheerleading tricks. The truck roared across the shallow ditch, over the bank and into the water.

She scrambled from the ditch, brushed off the dirt and began the long hike home. She'd have to tell Daddy he was right, Dick was just that, a dick. She would promise Daddy to never see him again.

And thank God she had spent all those hours loving CSI.

STARLIGHT VISION

She had hiked about ten miles that day and the tiredness seemed to creep up from her feet into her entire body. She shucked off the backpack. First things first. She gathered dried twigs and limbs scattered over the Mojave Desert sands and built a small fire.

A bottle of water and two strips of jerky became her supper. She sat with her ankles crossed, her face to the fire, and felt the night chill against her back.

I ought to get my jacket on, she thought. Instead, she turned sideways to the fire, stretched her legs out, lay back and looked up at the stars. The dry air brought them so close she felt she could reach up and pluck them as easily as she had picked muscadines or apples back home. The Milky Way spilled across the night heavens.

Not like back home where you never see a star, just neon flashing and a million car lights. Oh, my! There goes a meteor. Big one. Shucks. It burned out. Not like the one the night Tecumseh was born. His meteor is supposed to have gone from horizon to horizon. Ergo, Panther Across the Sky. The name fit, the way he led the tribes to fight like wildcats to preserve their lands and heritage.

She sensed movement, sat up and looked across the flames. A tall figure approached, his feet raising small puffs of dust. He wore buckskin with beads and porcupine quills decorating the shirt. Fringes on the sleeves and the edges of the pants swayed with his walk and the night breeze. Black hair showed faint touches of gray and hung in two long plaits.

"Ah—hello?" she said.

The Indian remained silent as he sat across from her. His face showed no emotions and she noticed the miles of ruts the years had gouged across his face.

She had thought she was alone as she hiked. Where had he come from? She started to speak, but he lifted a hand a few inches above his waist, palm toward her, and shook his head.

She remained silent as his gaze met hers. She felt as if he entered her mind through her eyes and controlled her thoughts. Her mind seemed to lift her above the desert, above her campfire, into the darkness while below her starlight flooded the desert. She could see beyond the edge of time and the end of distance.

Life harsh and bitter unrolled below her. Children slaughtered by soldiers. Children slaughtered by warriors. Laughter around campfires. Hunters strolling home with deer across their shoulders. Women sewing decorations onto deerskin tanned to a softness she felt against her skin. A boy running naked in a world of laugher and charging into a blue river. Line after line of horsemen, some armed with bows, some with firearms. Women laughing together as they rolled clay around space to create pottery. Bison skin covering a man who crawled on knees and one hand and carried a bow to within yards of a herd and released arrows that thunked into the chest of animal after animal. A tall bronze man sitting beside a fire, soldiers around him, one soldier kicking hot coals into his chest, the Indian leaping up, the soldiers shooting. Long lines of men, women and children walking in sun and rain while armed white men rode beside them. Images moved across the desert to the eastern forests and along rivers where she watched the timberlands disappear into cabins. Men with long muskets and rifles marched from settlements into native campgrounds and slaughtered natives. More frightening than all other images were the sight and sounds of a young woman being raped by soldiers.

As if a widescreen movie scene collapsed into a close-up, the young Indian woman reappeared with a baby in her arms. The baby drifted from her, expanded into an adult who, with a white man behind her, held another baby. The image repeated five times, with a white man behind each woman and each woman's completion lighter. The sixth woman, however, stood before an Indian, not a white man, and the seventh woman stood again in front of a white man. The last baby matured and aged into her grandmother's lined face and piercing black eyes.

Time and distance vanished.

Thunder rolled across the mountains and shook the air around her. She floated back to the ground. The campfire, now only embers, glowed but no longer offered heat. She shivered with cold. The Indian rose, nodded to her, and strode into the darkness. Dust rose with each step.

"Wait," she called. "Who are you? Are we—am I?"

He did not reply. He had vanished.

More lightning threw thunder rumbling and bumping from the mountains. Hair on her arms tingled. The next flash showed the landscape where he had walked devoid of all but rocks and cacti. Her mouth went dry. She looked toward the mountains, which stood black against the stars. She shook her head. No clouds. Just lightning and noise.

She rubbed her arms to wipe away the effects of the lightning. Took a deep breath and exhaled.

He can't have gone far.

She threw two small sticks on the embers and they swooshed into flame. She got up and in the firelight rummaged in her pack for her Petzl headlamp. She searched the ground the other side of the fire to find his tracks. The land was dusty. She could track him easily, find out who he was, where he came from, where he was going, if he were her ancestor. Or a dream.

But the desert had swallowed him without a sign. She zigzagged across the land where she had seen him walk, but as she circled back and forth, she found only her own tracks.

She decided she had dreamed the encounter and walked back to the fire.

An eagle feather and a broken arrow lay where he had been sitting.

THE BODYGUARD

"Bert, here's your first case," the assistant district attorney said to the newly hired law student. "Meet Jerry McKay, revenue agent. He'll brief you. I need you to go over the files and determine if we have a strong enough case to go to trial."

Bert rose from his desk chair and extended his hand to shake with Jerry, but the agent extended his right hand with the file. "Here's what I have," the agent said.

Bert thought Agent McKay was rude, but if he was as old as he looked, he probably had had his fill of chasing bad guys and didn't like the idea of some youngster deciding on his case.

The agent planted himself in the straight chair in front of Bert's desk. The second-year law student nodded, sat and opened the file.

Photographs on top. A stack of 8x10s, full color. He lifted the top picture. And stared at square cardboard containers, stacked two deep and strapped into units four by four on flats for ease of moving with a fork lift. Behind the containers stood a barn wall. Sunlight streamed between the ancient boards, and the camera had caught dust moats in the beams. An abandoned wasp nest withered in a corner.

"By God, no wonder Uncle Jeff made them move," he muttered. "And he used me for a bodyguard to boot."

"What?" the agent asked.

Bert smiled. "This could be a picture of my Uncle Jefferson's barn from more than twenty years go. I hadn't even given it a thought since that day. Until now."

He told the agent of that afternoon.

Uncle Jefferson drove up to the house in his 1955 Chevy pickup, red dust covering what blue and white paint had not turned to rust. Bert ran outside, clad in the overalls he had begged his mother for so he could dress just like Uncle Jefferson. Bert remembered he even had a red handkerchief hanging from his back pocket.

"Uncle Jeff," he hollered.

The old man opened his arms and knelt for the five-year-old to run into his hug. "Whatcha been doing, Bert?"

"Went fishing yesterday with Kevin from down the road. I caught three sunfish and mama cooked them for me for supper last night."

"You say? Well, boy, I'm proud for you. You want to come up to the house with me for a spell? We might go fishing down to the creek behind

my place, if you want to."

Bert turned, ran toward the house and yelled, *"Mama, Mama, can I go with Uncle Jefferson and go fishing?"*

Mama stepped onto the porch. Flour she dusted from her hands floated away on the breeze. *"You sure you want him this afternoon?"*

Jefferson nodded. *"I'll bring him back in time for supper, Louise."*

"That'll do. You can stay for supper if you want. You bring some fish and I'll fry up a hoe cake. Billy Joe will be glad to see you. It's been a spell."

"How's he doing at his job down at the mill?"

"Oh, fine. Just long days and a long walk up the hill to home. You don't be late, ya hear?"

"Be back with Bert about dark."

Bert grabbed his uncle's hand and skipped to keep up with the long steps of his six-foot-four idol.

At Jefferson's house, instead of going inside, Jefferson headed for the barn behind the house and on the other side of the garden.

"Where we going?" Bert asked.

"Just to the barn. I put our fishing poles in there."

Jefferson pushed open the right-hand double door and led the boy into the dimness. Sunlight sliced through spaces between the wall boards. Dust floated in the beams. The barn could have been used as a garage for six cars between the stalls along the two sides where Jefferson kept his mules back when he plowed by hand. Now they stood empty. Only an old International Harvester tractor, as rusty as Uncle Jeff's old truck, stood in the barn. Behind the tractor, Bert saw three men and something stacked.

The men stared at them. Jefferson walked around the tractor and toward them. *"Hello, boys,"* Jefferson said.

The men nodded. One said, *"Hello, Jefferson. What you bringing that boy in here for? He ain't even your boy."*

"No, he's not my own but he is mine. He's my favorite nephew and we fish together a lot. We're going fishing this afternoon. I have to get my poles and gear from inside that stall at the back yonder."

He headed toward the stall. *"Come on, Bert. You need to pick out which of the poles you're going to use."*

Bert trotted beside Jefferson.

When Jefferson stopped a few feet from the men, Bert also stopped. Jefferson pulled a bag of tobacco and papers from his overall bib pocket.

He seemed to forget both the men and Bert as he concentrated on building his cigarette. With tobacco on the paper, he pulled the string with his teeth to close the tobacco bag, stuffed it and the folder of paper back into his overall pocket. He rolled the paper around the leaf and licked the edge. He slid a finger along the seal and placed the end of the cigarette between his lips. He pulled a kitchen match from the same chest pocket of his overalls and struck it on the back of his pants leg.

He lit the cigarette and exhaled the smoke through his nose. He coughed softly. "You boys going to be coming here much? I don't think Bert needs to get involved with this. How you fellows feel about that?"

No one answered. Bert wondered why one of the men balled up his fists and took a step forward, only to be pulled back by one of the others.

Jefferson looked at the abandoned wasp nest behind the men. He took three more puffs from the cigarette and dropped it onto the dirt floor of the barn. He reached down for Bert's hand and said, "Come on, let's get them fishing poles."

The old man and the boy passed the men and their stack of boxes. Bert wondered what was inside. All he could see was the label that said Mason Jars, Quart. He wondered if the men had canned some garden tomatoes or made pickles like his mama did in quart Mason jars.

He tagged along with Jefferson as they went into the stall and selected two cane poles each. As they came out, Bert noticed one of the men was stomping his brogan on the smoking cigarette.

"Uncle Jefferson, you didn't put out your cigarette," Bert said.

Jefferson replied, "Well, I'll be darned. So I didn't. I guess I better be more careful when I come in to work on the tractor this week. Don't want to set the barn on fire. Come on, Bert, let's get to the creek. I got a Mason jar there and we can scratch us up some worms and keep 'em in the jar."

While they fished, Bert heard noises from back toward the house and barn. It was almost dark when they came up the hill from the creek, Jefferson toting a string of bream and cats.

"Let me check the barn," Jefferson said and looked inside. "Well, those ole boys understood and took their work somewhere else to hide it. Let's go get these fish fried and eat some of your mama's hoecake. Knowing her, she made biscuits too and we can have them for dessert with her cane syrup."

Bert ended his story and laughed.

"What's so funny?" McKay asked.

"I just realized Uncle Jeff used me as a bodyguard when I was five. I was his protection when he threw a group of bootleggers off his place. Even the roughest bootleggers in Georgia won't kill a man in front of a child."

"Yeah. Well, these I caught are tough. What'd you say your uncle's name is?"

"Jefferson Rogers. He died last summer. The farm is empty now. Waiting for the estate to settle."

"Uh-huh. Well, I hate to tell you, but that picture was taken in his barn three days ago. I reckon those same fellas came back."

THE 4-H CLUB

Jerry was delighted when the teacher announced they were going to form a 4-H club at Jefferson Primary School in Tickleboro.

"We have seven acres you can use for our projects," Mrs. Sanger stated.

He raised his hand. "May my project be goats?"

"Any animal you want."

Another hand went up. "I want mine to be snakes. I love them and mama said I can't keep them in the house," Jason said.

"Well, we'll have to see about that. You'll have to make some snake-proof houses for them. It may get too cold this winter to keep them outside."

"Can't I use the classroom if I just keep a few?"

She shook her head. Snakes in her classroom. *I don't think so.*

"We'll just have to see," she repeated.

"Could I have shoats for my project?" Benny called from the back of the room. He did not bother to raise his hand. But she wasn't surprised. He never raised his hand.

"I don't see why not. I think the shoats and the goats will get along just fine."

Laugher rippled through the class and someone said, "Shoats and goats." The class in unison chanted "Shoats and goats. Shoats and goats."

Mrs. Sanger laughed with them. After a minute, she lifted her hand and said, still smiling, "Okay, class, let's get back to projects."

The rest of the hour was consumed as various students suggested ideas for their projects. When the bell rang, students grabbed up their books as usual, but instead of running out they collected in small groups and chatted about their projects.

Mrs. Sanger noticed the town children and the country kids, as usual, gathered in separate groups. She had hoped this common interest would unite them and some might even want to share a project. *Oh, well, so be it. As small as Tickleboro is, the town kids think they are better. It's about time we had a 4-H Club. Now I have to investigate what to do to get ours into the national organization.*

She knew Her Honor The Mayor Mrs. Anderson would not usually spring for anything she considered wasteful. But maybe, just may, she would spring for fencing around the land for the animals. The students could provide the labor. Some of the farm boys would be able to bring in their tools.

She gathered up her papers, stuffed them into her briefcase, left the school grounds and strode down the six blocks to the mayor's office. Mrs. Anderson was in.

"Good afternoon, Betty. What brings you here? Is everything okay down at the school?"

"All is well, Madam Mayor."

Mrs. Anderson waved her right hand forward. "Oh, poo, Betty. Since when did classmates have to be that formal? Besides, you're the one who ranked tops in our class. I was near the bottom."

Betty smiled. "Maybe so. But you and Ike moved right to the top. Like Eisenhower, you've got smarts that a lot of us don't have. What I want to talk to you about is I'm forming a 4-H club for our students. Is there something in our budget that will pay for a hog-wire fence around those seven acres beside the school where they can keep their animals? Some of them don't have space at their homes for a calf or goats." She grinned. "Or shoats."

"Goats and shoats?" The mayor laughed. "I'll find the money somewhere. We have an emergency fund outside the school budget. I'll get the council to okay it. You've got a good idea. Just get me an itemized cost estimate. Fence, posts, staples, labor. Will the labor provide tools? How much can the boys do themselves? Talk to that new fella who's organizing a scout troop over in Pendale and see if some of them will help as one of their projects."

"I'll get right on it."

The hardware store was still open, and Jake listed the cost of hog-wire per 100 feet, the number of posts and their cost, and the pounds of staples needed. "You'll have to measure your perimeters and figure from that."

Next afternoon, the students stayed and measured. The girls tried to help, but the boys kept telling them they were only girls and this was man's work. The boys' attitudes didn't seem to dampen the girls' excitement.

"I can bring in our wire stretchers. We got one for hog-wire. And Daddy said I can bring in two of his hammers," Bea said.

"I can nail staples in," another girl offered.

Jerry halted half-way across one side of the field, threw both hands up and let fly the measuring tape. He stared at the girls. "We got posthole diggers. And I can dig postholes." He turned around, realized he had dropped the tape, bent, picked it up, and continued down the side of the meadow.

The farm boys were as excited as the town boys. At home, they had to pitch in with farm chores and had no special animals of their own to tend to.

"My pa said he'd help. We got a posthole digger he uses on the tractor. It shore does beat using them hand ones."

"*Those*, Billy. *Those*."

"Those what, Ma'am?"

"Not 'them hand ones.' 'Those hand ones.'"

He shrugged.

The measurement completed, the children started for home, the boys chanting about "goats and shoats." The girls were a bit quieter, but she heard three farm girls talking about rabbits.

Jollie, one of the town girls, surprised her when she hung back as the others left and asked if she would be able to have a calf as her project. "I think they are soooo prudy."

Mrs. Sanger assured Jollie she could pick her own project. And a calf would be just fine if her father said okay and would buy her one. The child skipped home.

A week later, the fence was up and an L-shaped lean-to stood in the northwest corner to provide animals shelter against the winter winds. "Not that it gets that cold here," one of the fathers said as he helped build it. "But better to be sure."

Saturday found goats and shoats established in the pen. The girls dragged their fathers back to build a rabbit hutch large enough for all three girls to have three pens each. It paralleled the lean-to, its solid back to the north.

"Will they get too hot in summer?" Beth asked.

Mrs. Sanger assured her that the sweetgum tree, now leafless for the winter, would provide shade for the hutch.

A week passed. Children stayed after school to tend to their animals. Mrs. Sanger was first to school on Monday and noticed the gate to the pasture was open.

"Oh dear Gussie! Where are the goats and shoats?"

She ran to the door and down the hall to the principal's office to call the sheriff to send deputies to help find the animals. The children would be heartbroken.

She halted on the stoop. The door was ajar. Who in the world left the door open? The janitor? Had he come to work drunk again and for the tenth time forgotten to lock up?

She took a deep breath and stepped inside.

The smell hit her. "Goats and shoats," she muttered.

First room, one of the goats stood on the teacher's desk. The papers Mrs. French had left were scattered on the floor, where one of the shoats rooted them around.

She watched a moment, then circled the room to run them into the hall. The shoat grunted and trotted away, but, reluctant to leave his game, swung around her. The goat leaped from the desk, shook his head, and trotted through the door. She ran at the shoat, and it fled the screaming maniac.

She slammed the door behind her and headed down the hall. Mr. Wilson had left his coat, a London Fog, hanging on the coat rack inside his classroom. One of the goats had pulled it to the floor and discovered it was edible. He and the shoat were sharing it.

She backed into the hall and met Jason's pet slithering toward her.

She screamed loud enough to have drowned out all of the cannons at Gettysburg and ran toward the front door.

She collided with Mr. Wilson. He staggered back.

"My God, Betty. What's the matter?"

Mrs. Sanger leaped away, her face flaming with embarrassment. She pointed down the hallway and stammered, "Our 4-H project has become 4-H all right. Four HELLS, and damnation to boot. Goats and shoats are headed for the barbeque pit. And I'm gonna take a hoe to that snake."

Wilson smiled. "Could we have fried snake and rabbit stew with the barbecue?"

SMART-PHONE MESSAGES

She tore out of the house, like Dagwood Bumstead of the comics, late as usual and in too much of a hurry for a goodbye kiss. He shook his head and started toward his office and typewriter to work on the novel he was basing on a ten-year-old triple-murder cold case he recently solved. If he could just finish it on schedule and his agent was right, it might go into a movie and he could retire.

Hope she doesn't get caught speeding. I'll have to use up a few more favors to get her out of it. She and Sally just might not make it to the opera in time to get seated.

He was glad Sally agreed to use his ticket. He had rather be tied to a bed post and lashed with a bull whip than to go the opera. As he walked through the living room, he spotted her android phone, abandoned on the coffee table. He picked it up and shoved it into the cargo pocket on his left side. His was in his right-hand pocket.

He was deep into *Chapter Three* and the first illicit meeting between the housewife and the detective when her phone beeped to signify a message. He removed the phone, took it to the kitchen, laid it on the counter and returned to his writing.

The phone beeped again, this time the sound bouncing off the counter. He ignored it, but the third time it beeped, he got up and went to answer it. Just in case.

Must be something important, he thought. A police detective, he never left his phone unanswered or messages ignored. He looked.

The circle without a face showed she had three messages. A fourth came in as he looked. He clicked onto Facebook and onto the lightning bolt to reveal a column of new messages from Midnight Warrior.

Where are you?
You haven't answered. You promised.
Call me Please.
What have I done that you won't answer me?

He stared at the messages. *Must be some sort of mistake her leaving the phone. Who the heck is Midnight Warrior? She never mentioned anyone like that. But then, if she's having an affair…*

My God, what made me think she's having an affair? It can't be. No, of course not. Maybe because of what I'm writing. No. I'd know if she were stepping out. But just in case…

He backed up the message box as far as it went, to the beginning of messages. And read. He sat down at the kitchen table, unable to read more than the first few entries.

Let's have lunch.
Meet me at Sharpy's. One.
Will do.

Loved seeing you.
Me too.
Let's lunch again.
Okay.
Maybe at the Oyster Bar? I got a lot to talk about.

He took a deep breath and looked at the overhead light. *The Oyster Bar? That's where I met her. How dare her sneak off there to meet a lover.*

Got room 13 at Sleepy Hollow for the week. Meet there? Decide on where?

He voiced his thoughts. "My God, right next door to the Oyster Bar. It is an affair." He read on.

Why not? We won't be bothered there. Twelve?
Yes.

Wonderful time getting to know you. See you tomorrow I hope?
Indeed. Same time, same station.
I'll get you a key tomorrow.
Okay. See you at noon.
Are you going to tell him?
I want to. But I can't. At least not now. He'll have problems with you.
I understand. I was afraid you might. But he should know.

"I'll kill her." He paced the floor and spoke to the walls. "Or maybe him. This has been going on for a week and I didn't realize—hell and damn. Ethel must have forgotten to tell lover boy she was going to the opera. We're too old to be having affairs. My God, maybe she's having the midlife crisis men are supposed to have."

The phone throbbed in his hand and indicated another message.

Where are you? I thought you were coming over tonight.

He messaged: "I'll tell you at the Sleepy Hollow. I'll be there in a few minutes. Hubby's gone to the opera." *And you're going to your own funeral.*

Instant reply. *Be there in twenty. Just getting a burger.*

He slipped on his shoulder holster before he left home and headed to the motel, Ethel's phone in hand. At the motel, he parked away from Room 13 and waited for lover boy to arrive. An SUV pulled up in front of the motel and a long-legged woman stepped out and entered Room 13. The inside lights flicked on, and the woman stood at the partially open curtains and looked at the parking lot. She wore blue jeans and a cotton shirt open at the throat. He had seen hiking boots as she strode from her car.

He sat in the car and shivered with loss and fury. *A damn dike. She's having an affair with a damn dike.*

He pulled the phone out of his pocket and messaged. *In hubby's car. Are you there?*

Just got here. Knock the "shave and haircut" and I'll open the door.

He backed out, drove to the end of the parking lot where she couldn't see him from her room. He turned around, drove back, and parked in front of her room. He stepped from the car, took his pistol from his shoulder holster and shoved it under the driver's seat. *I can't afford to kill her. I'll just get her out of town.*

He locked the car, dropped the key into his pocket and approached the door to Room 13.

He knocked to the rhythm of *shave and a haircut, two bits*. The door opened.

He pushed his way inside.

"Who are *you*?" the woman demanded.

"I'm her husband. Who the hell do you think you are and what the hell do you think you and my wife doing?"

"You're Dixon?"

He nodded his gray head. "You're damn right I am."

"She didn't want to tell you."

"Oh, I'm sure of that. She didn't want me to find out, either. Thirty years and she steps out on me with a dike. I—I feel like killing you both."

The woman pulled a chair out from the table. "Sit," she said. "It's not what you think."

"Yeah? What am I supposed to think? The two of you sneaking off to a motel day after day for how long? You gotta be—Ethel's old enough to be your mother—"

Dixon sat and buried his face in his hands. "I can't believe she's leaving me for a dike."

"She's not leaving you. Please don't think that."

He looked up. "What the hell am I supposed to think? I saw the messages. You—you and Ethel... I can't believe it."

"Look, it's time you knew. She didn't want to tell you."

"I'm sure she didn't want me to know. Why else is she sneaking off to have sex in the middle of the day? With a dike, no less."

The woman laughed. "You got to be kidding. You thought—? My lord, I see now why you're so mad."

"It's no laughing matter."

"No," she frowned. "No, it's serious. Look at me. Do I look familiar at all?"

He studied her face and then he saw. "My God, you look like Ethel."

"I'm the grown-up baby she gave away. Remember? You were both teenagers and you got her pregnant. She was afraid to tell you, afraid you might blame her genes because I'm a lesbian. But I'm not your wife's lover, I'm her daughter. And yours."

THE NIGHT PEOPLE

Kenzie was out of cigarettes. Not good for a chain smoker at a little after ten at night. She left her apartment for the drug store, four blocks along Cambridge Avenue, then a right onto First and a left onto River Road to the Walgreen's.

While there, she figured she might as well grab a bottle of diet Coke. She paid, stuck the pack of Winstons into her jacket pocket and slipped her arm through the handles of the plastic bag with the Coke.

She heard footsteps behind her when she turned off River onto First, but figured whoever it was would turn into one of the many apartment buildings. But the walker stayed behind her when she turned onto her street—Cambridge Avenue. Four blocks to her building.

One block, cross the street and continue on. Three more blocks. All dark. The one street light had died last week and not been replaced. She picked up her pace. The footsteps behind matched her steps.

Fear crept into her. Alone, no one knew she was out. *I should-a called Martha to let her know. To plan to call her when I got back.*

She reached another corner, stopped for a car to pass. The footsteps behind her also stopped. She looked back and saw a dark-clad figure about half a block away, his back to her. A light flickered—a cigarette lighter. He had turned his back to the night wind to light a cigarette.

She hurried on. The footsteps picked up again. The wind lifted a discarded page from the *Globe* and tossed it into her path. She shivered and hurried on.

At the final cross street, she scooted across and almost trotted the last thirty feet to her apartment door.

She had her keys in her hand to open the outside door and pushed herself into the inner hallway, turned and shoved the outside door closed. Her free hand trembled.

The figure reached the outside door, lifted a hand in greeting and smiled.

She dropped her house keys and fumbled on the floor to grab them. Standing back up, she gripped the bag with the Coke bottle and prepared to swing it.

He held a key ring in his right hand, shoved a key into the lock and entered.

She drew her arm back, "Oh, please, Ma'am. I didn't mean to scare you. I live in the third-floor apartment."

Color gradually returned to Kenzie's face. She lowered the makeshift weapon.

"You about scared the dickens out of me. I thought you were following me. Please don't ever do that again."

He reached beyond her with his keys, opened the inside door, and held the door for her.

"I apologize. I tried to stay back when I realized you seemed nervous. I'll be more aware in the future. But this is a pretty safe neighborhood."

She nodded, passed him, and headed down the hall to her apartment that backed onto the alley. "Good night," she called over her shoulder.

He echoed her words and she heard his shoes slipping up the stairs.

Relieved, she let herself into her efficiency apartment.

Coke wasn't gonna settle her nerves. She went into the kitchen, found a half-bottle of Bourbon, and poured four fingers into a water glass. *One of these days, I'm gonna get some real cocktail glasses.*

After the walk, the room seemed stuffy, and she opened the window on the right side of the room into the alley. She opened the other alley window and hoped for a cross breeze. These northern cities never heard of air conditioning. First floor, but no fear with the iron bars only four inches apart to prevent anyone crawling in.

In an attempt to put the walk from her mind, she picked up a book, kicked off her tennis shoes, and settled down to read. The quiet wrapped around her and before she finished her drink, she began to doze and the book fell into her lap. *Time to sack out.*

She pulled off her jeans, shucked out of her cotton shirt and bra, pulled on a tee shirt, and crawled into the bed. She clicked off the light.

What's that noise? Something in the alley?

She eased from the bed in the dark and stepped across the room to the left-side alley window. She leaned forward and pulled the curtains slightly open.

A face stared at her.

She screamed.

The man ran.

She slammed the window down, jerked the drapes closed and ran to the bedside phone. She felt for the dial in the dark, but was unable to figure where the 911 numbers were. She flicked on her light, pushed the emergency numbers and turned the light off.

"Nine-one-one, what is your emergency?"

"Get the police."

"Alright."

A moment, then, "Police. May I help you?"

Kenzie still blubbered, but managed to give her name and address and tell them to hurry and catch the Peeping Tom.

"An officer lives in your building. I'll call him."

She heard footsteps running down the stairs and out the front door. A few minutes later, when the knock came on her door she held the kitchen butcher knife in her hand.

"Who's there?"

"Police. You called?"

"Did you catch him?"

"No. I need to talk to you, to take a report. May I come in?"

"No. How do I know you're the police?"

"Ma'am, my badge number is 7893. My name is Lawrence Pilcher. Call headquarters and they can verify who I am."

She called the operator again, got transferred to the station, gave the information and was told yes, Officer Pilcher had been sent to answer her call.

She opened the door. The knife was still in her hand. She gawked. The man was the one who followed her home only a short while ago. He wore a Red Sox tee shirt and jeans, not a uniform.

"You?" she stammered. "You are a policeman?"

"Yes, Ma'am. Would you mind putting that knife away? Please?"

She looked at the knife. "I'm sorry. I was just plain out scared."

She carried the knife into her kitchen while Pilcher stood in her doorway. He remained standing while she told him what happened and he took notes.

She pointed to the window where the man had been. "I heard a noise, and when I went to look out he was right there. His face wasn't more than three inches from me."

Pilcher walked to the window, pulled back the heavy drapes and looked out. He shook his head, and with no comment he walked to the other window and looked out.

He asked for a description of the man, but all she was able to tell him was that he needed a shave and had big eyes.

"We've had reports of a Peeping Tom in the area. Sounds like the same man. Unshaven is all anybody has been able to say. You keep your windows down. If you have a fan, run it to keep cool. But don't open your windows or the drapes no matter what. Call the operator if you get scared and I'll come down. I'll be outside for a while, walking the area, Maybe an hour or more."

"Thank you so much, Officer," she said.

He left and she crawled into bed again. In a few minutes, she got up and went to the window away from the Peeping Tom and opened it about six inches. Cool air drifted in with the drapes open, but as soon as she pulled them closed, the breeze died. She tossed for a while, turning over the two events in her mind and grateful to have a policeman in the building. In spite of the heat, she fell asleep.

Well after midnight, voices woke her. She sat up in bed and listened. The words were almost inaudible. Curiosity got to her, and she crept as quiet as a cat to the still-open window, across from the one she slammed in the face of the peeper.

And heard more than she wanted to.

"Keep it down, Larry. We don't want to wake up the neighborhood."

She knelt on the floor and eased an opening between the curtains. A truck sat in the alley, a covered delivery truck with no lettering on the side. Men moved from the back door of the building across the alley to the truck and passed coats to someone inside.

"Damned if they aren't robbing the clothing store," she whispered. "I better call the cops."

She crawled to the phone, lifted the receiver, and halted. Their voices had awakened her. Her voice would warn them. Not just warn them that the police were on the way, but tell him who was calling. Even one of those new-fangled cell phones wouldn't do any good—they'd still be able to hear her. She eased the phone back onto the receiver.

"I gotta get out of this place. I'm gonna give my notice first thing tomorrow, lease or not. I can't handle all these goings on."

She crawled back to the window and watched through the crack in the curtains. Half an hour later, one of the men said, "There ain't another thing worth hauling out of there. Let's get going afore somebody wakes up."

She leaned into the window bars in an attempt to read the tag number, but realized there was no tag. The truck drove off. She went back to bed.

Morning came and she woke to the sound of shouts in the alley. She went to the window, stood off to the side and listened.

"They took it all out the back door. Look. They dropped some coat hangers."

She backed away. She didn't want to be seen and connected in any way with the burglary. She waited impatiently for nine o'clock to call and inform the landlord she was moving. The secretary said he would not be in the office until Monday.

"I have to move," she said, and told the secretary about the Peeping Tom and that the policeman said the Peeping Tom had been around for weeks.

"You have a lease," she replied. "You can't just move."

"I can. This place is creepy. A Peeping Tom last night. A man following me home from the store and scaring me half to death. And now *Larry* and his buddies breaking in the department store across the alley and waking me up in the middle of the night. I watched them empty the store and my phone was so close to the window I didn't dare call the police. This place is not safe. I'm moving before something else happens."

She hung up. Her hands trembled. She fought to keep from crying.

She was still wiping tears when the phone rang. The landlord. "Lady, you have a lease. If you move before it runs out, I'll take you to court for the rent for the next four months. So don't think you are going anywhere. And why do you think somebody named Larry was the burglar across the alley? Did you call the police?"

"No, I did not call the police. Like I told your secretary, my phone was right at the window. I heard them call somebody Larry is how I know the name. And I'm going to move as soon as—"

But he had disconnected.

She didn't own much. The apartment came furnished. She had clothes and a few dishes and a ten-inch black-and-white TV with rabbit ears. She began to pack. He'd have to find her.

She heard someone trotting down the stairs. The footsteps approached her door. Someone knocked. "Yeah? Who is it?" she called.

"It's Officer Pilcher. From upstairs."

She opened the door to find his pistol pointed to her face. Her last thought as his gun fired was Officer Lawrence Pilcher was Larry from the alley last night.

THE JUDAS GOAT

"I found a cave," Will said as he ran into the barn where the old man who worked for his father was shoeing a horse. "I came to get the lantern. I'm gonna explore it. "

The old man dropped the horse's leg and stood straight, the rasp clutched in his right hand. He shook it at Will. "No, I don't think so, son." He emphasized the *no* but continued as if only curious. "Where abouts is it?"

"It's on the east side on No-Name Mountain. I saw a huge old mountain goat high up and it disappeared. I went up to see where it had gone. There's a big opening there. I can't wait to get inside. I'll take a long string to unroll behind me. I hope it's a cavern, you know, with stalactites and crystals and such." Will headed off toward the empty stall where they kept odds and ends of supplies they seldom or no longer used on the ranch.

"*No*, Will," the old man called after him. "Don't go in that cave. No one has ever come out. I knew two men who went up there years ago. They followed the Judas Goat and neither one of them came back. They just vanished."

"What's a Judas goat?"

"It's what the sheep herders call the goat they put a bell on and the sheep just follow it right into the slaughter house. You follow that Judas goat, ain't no telling what'll happen to you. Don't go up there. You'll never come back. Mr. Jefferson'll kill me if I let you go up there and disappear like Luke and Jake."

"Didn't anybody go looking for them?"

The old man shook his head. "No. It was dangerous. Everybody knows there's something there, but nobody knows what. And nobody wants to go find out. You find out, you never come back to tell."

"I'll come back," the youth grinned.

"Just because you've been to college and have all that book learning doesn't mean anything out here. You don't know this land and what it holds. You've been here, what? Four months since your mom died and you came from Chicago to live with your dad? No. You talk to your dad before you go back on that mountain."

Will shrugged and said, "Okay."

But he didn't mention it to his father. Instead he sat on the porch and watched the barn. As soon as the old man left for his own cabin for lunch, Will scooted to the barn and grabbed a battery-powered lantern and a large ball of twine waiting to be used to mark a fence line for post holes.

I'll show the old man there's nothing to be scared of in that cave. And I'll find out what the big mystery is all about. Just might make me famous, too, when I come back with all the information about the cave.

He drove his father's Honda four-wheeler down the trail, parked it as close to No-Name Mountain as he could, and headed up the rocky incline, lantern in one hand, string in the other. He locked his mind on what he wanted to find: Stalactites and stalagmites, quartz crystals, Indian pottery from the days of the Anasazi. Maybe even something left by the Spanish centuries ago. Gold maybe. Or maybe something like the Dead Sea Scrolls stuffed into pottery. No one had ever come out with the secrets.

Excitement drove him as he scrambled over the rocks. From overhead, a rock tumbled down to his left. He watched it a moment and looked up to see what had caused it to fall. The white billy scooted along the ridge.

Well, that goat came out and I will too. If the cave doesn't eat goats, it surely can't eat me.

He paused at the entrance only long enough to tie one end of the ball of twine to a bush and to light the lantern. He entered, and as the light from the entrance faded, he held the lantern aloft to see better.

So far, nothing but black stone walls and hard solid stone underfoot. Even the ceiling was solid stone. No crystals. No limestone formations from seeping water.

Will was careful to control the ball of twine, but wondered why he bothered. He had not seen any side tunnels.

I could just leave it he thought and laid it down. But after another 100 yards he came to a fork. He went back for the twine and unrolled it as he went down the left-hand fork. *I'm a lefty, so I'll stick with the left-hand forks*, he promised himself.

The fork ended in a cavern, but the thirty-foot diameter room had no other exit. He wandered around it and searched the walls, but could find no sign of an exit.

Back he went, trying to roll up the twine and carry the lantern. He finally just cut this string with his pocket knife. *Glad Dad gave it to me first thing after I got here. I thought it was kinda silly at the time, but it sure is handy now.*

At the junction he tied the strings together and started down the right-hand tunnel. No more forks for another five hundred yards, when the cord gave out. He dropped the cardboard center and walked down the left-hand tunnel.

Light appeared thirty minutes later. Faint, but brighter as he moved along.

It's not a cave; it's a tunnel, just a tunnel through the mountain.

He stepped out onto a large platform and stood near the edge. The sun warmed his face but a cool breeze kept the warmth comfortable. *It's a lot cooler inside the tunnel than outside.*

Off to his right he saw an opening in the brush and headed toward the path. He had taken only six steps when a female voice behind him said, "Who are you and why are you here?"

He spun around, to face a young dark-skinned woman and the arrow she held at full draw, its blade pointed at him. She wore only a long dress of some sort of hide that he thought looked like suede. A quiver hung down her back from a strap over her shoulder.

"I...I—hey, don't shoot me with that thing. You could kill me."

"Why are you here?"

"I found the cave. I wanted to know what was in it."

"You found out. Now, let's go. Take the trail down the hill."

He looked down the hill. The valley stretched into the distance beyond his ability to focus on that lay there. But in between grew crops. He recognized corn because of its height. Cattle fed in an area of many acres off to his left, behind a rail fence. Flowing water beyond the cattle reflected the sunlight into his eyes.

I thought a fence had to have at least three or four layers of logs but this one doesn't have but two. Maybe the cows are trained.

In the distance people milled around small fires. What little smoke drifted upward vanished before it rose fifty feet. He frowned. *What are those openings? Cliff dwellings? I can't tell, the shadow of that overhanging cliff is too heavy. People live here?*

"You live here?" he asked. "It looks like a bunch of cliff homes up there." *This must be where the Anasazi disappeared to.* He pointed.

She replied. "Yes, I live here. Go ahead down the pathway."

She eased pressure off the bow, removed the arrow and slipped it into the quiver. "You'll be a welcome guest. No need for the bow now." She extended her arm to indicate for him to lead the way down the path.

"Great," he replied and strode ahead of her. His stride bounced with excitement. He would be the first person to visit this cliff village and return home to tell about his discovery.

At the base of the hill, two men waited. Like the girl, they were dressed as he thought the early American Indians dressed—the men in loin cloths of what also looked like suede. None wore any type of foot covering.

At first glance, he was convinced he had found the Anasazi, but as he approached closer, he realized one of the men's complexion matched the girl's coloration, black hair and dark eyes, but the other man was blond and had blue eyes.

Nope, can't be the Anasazi unless some white folks found them too and stayed on.

Halfway to the village, he stopped. *Stayed on? The men who came up here and never were found…. Did they stay on? Did they want to stay here? I don't want to stay here, I want to go home. To tell what I've found.*

"Something wrong?" the girl asked.

"No, but I think I'll go back home. You don't need to entertain me. But first, tell me, are you the Anasazi? The lost tribe of Indians?"

"Only our family members know our history. You can learn when you join one of the families."

"*Oh no.* I don't want to join one of your families. I think I'll go back home now."

The blond man took his arm. "No, you don't leave. No one leaves. We can't have the secret out. It would be the end of us all if the outside world discovered us. You are here to stay."

Will jerked him arm free and darted back up the hill. He had not gone twenty yards when he was brought down with a tackle that would have pleased any football coach. As he fell, he extended his arms and his own football training led him to bend his elbows as his hands hit, but his face slammed into the dirt.

He raised his head and coughed as blood ran from his nose. He pushed himself up onto hands and knees and sat. He tried to wipe the blood from his face with his shirttail.

"Tilt your head just a little and pinch your nose. Breathe through your mouth. It'll stop in a minute," the blond man suggested.

Will sat silent for a few minutes and the bleeding stopped. He rose and glared at the white man.

"You can't keep me here," Will growled. "They know where I am.

They'll come for me."

The blue-eyed man smiled. "I used to think so too, Half-pint, but nobody knows we're here. Not even your dad."

Will frowned. "How'd you know my nickname? I haven't been called that in years." He wiped the last of the blood from his face with his shirt sleeve.

"You look just like your dad."

"He'll find me."

"No. We aren't on any map. We're off all flight lanes, and any cross-country plane that might venture overhead is too high to see inside this valley. And anybody else who decides to venture into here stays. Besides, we'll close the entrance again. It was only open to let in a few more game. No one finds the entrance until we need more meat—or a larger gene pool.

"Your dad called me Luke. Here, I carry the name of Deerslayer. Welcome to your new home."